Butterfly

Also by Virginia Andrews ®

Butterfly

The New Virginia Andrews®

POCKET
BOOKS

LONDON • SYDNEY • NEW YORK • TOKYO • SINGAPORE • TORONTO

First published in Great Britain by Pocket Books, 1999
An imprint of Simon & Schuster UK Ltd
A Viacom Company

1 3 5 7 9 10 8 6 4 2

Simon & Schuster UK Ltd
Africa House
64-78 Kingsway
London WC2B 6AH

Simon & Schuster Australia
Sydney

A CIP catalogue record for this book is available from the British Library

ISBN 0-671-02197-4

Printed and bound in Great Britain by
Caledonian International Book Manufacturing, Glasgow.

Prologue

I was alone in Mrs. McGuire's office, waiting to meet the couple who had asked to see me. Sitting "properly" on the straight-back chair next to Mrs. McGuire's desk was making my back ache but I knew from past experience that I had better be on my best behavior. Mrs. McGuire was the chief administrator of our orphanage and pounced on us if we slouched or did anything else "improper" in front of visitors.

"Posture, posture," she would cry out when she passed us in the cafeteria, and we all would snap to attention. Those who didn't obey her had to walk around with a book on their heads for hours, and if the book fell off, they would have to do it over again the next day.

"You children are orphans," she lectured to us, "looking for some nice people to come snatch you up and make you members of their families. You must be better than other children, children with parents and homes. You must be healthier, smarter, more polite, and most certainly more respectful. In short," she said in a voice that often turned shrill during her endless speeches, "you must become desirable. Why," she asked, sweeping her eyes over each and every one of us critically, her thin lips pursed, "would anyone want you to be their daughter or son?"

She was right. Who would ever want me? I thought. I was born prematurely. Some of the boys and girls here said I was stunted. Just yesterday, Donald Lawson called me the Dwarf.

"Even when you're in high school, you'll wear little-girl clothes," he taunted.

He strutted away with his head high, and I could tell it made him feel better to make me feel bad. My tears were like trophies for him, and the sight of them didn't make him feel sorry. Instead, they encouraged him.

"Even your tears are tiny," he sang as he walked down the hall. "Maybe we should call you Tiny Tears instead of the Dwarf."

The kids at the orphanage weren't the only ones who thought there was something wrong with me, though. Margaret Lester, who was the tallest girl in the orphanage, fourteen with legs that seemed to reach up to her shoulders, overheard the last couple I'd met talking about me and couldn't wait to tell me all the horrible things they had to say.

"The man said he thought you were adorable, but when they found out how old you were, they wondered why you were so small. She thought you might be sickly and then they decided to look at someone else," Margaret told me with a twisted smirk on her face.

No potential parents ever looked at her, so she was happy when one of us was rejected.

"I'm not sickly," I whispered in my own defense. "I haven't even had a cold all year."

I always spoke in a soft, low voice and then, when I was made to repeat something, I struggled to make my voice louder. Mrs. McGuire said I had to appear more self-assured.

"It's fine to be a little shy, Janet," she told me. "Goodness knows, most children today are too loud and obnoxious, but if you're too modest, people will pass you over. They'll think you're withdrawn, like a turtle more comfortable in his shell. You don't want that, do you?"

I shook my head but she continued her lecture.

"Then stand straight when you speak to people and look at them and not at the floor. And don't twist your fingers around each other like that. Get your shoulders back. You need all the height you can achieve."

When I had come to her office today, she had me sit in this chair and then paced in front of me, her high heels clicking like little hammers on the tile floor as she advised and directed me on how to behave once the Delorices arrived. That was their names, Sanford and Celine Delorice. Of course, I hadn't set eyes on them before. Mrs. McGuire told me, however, that they had seen me a number of times. That came as a surprise. A number of times? I wondered when, and if that was true, why had I never seen them?

"They know a great deal about you, Janet, and still they are interested. This is your best opportunity yet. Do you understand?" she asked, pausing to look at me. "Straighten up," she snapped.

I did so quickly.

"Yes, Mrs. McGuire," I said.

"What?" She put her hand behind her ear and leaned toward me. "Did you say something, Janet?"

"Yes, Mrs. McGuire."

"Yes what?" she demanded, standing back, her hands on her hips.

"Yes, I understand this is my best opportunity, Mrs. McGuire."

"Good, good. Keep your voice strong and clear. Speak only when you're spoken to, and smile as much as you can. Don't spread your legs too far apart. That's it. Let me see your hands," she demanded, reaching out to seize them in her own long, bony fingers.

She turned my hands over so roughly my wrists stung.

"Good," she said. "You do take good care of yourself, Janet. I think that's a big plus for you. Some of our children, as you know, think they are allergic to bathing."

She glanced at the clock.

"They should be arriving soon. I'm going out front to greet them. Wait here and when we come through the door, stand up to greet us. Do you understand?"

"Yes, Mrs. McGuire." Her hand went behind her ear again. I cleared my throat and tried again. "Yes, Mrs. McGuire."

She shook her head and looked very sad, her eyes full of doubt.

"This is your big chance, your best chance, Janet. Maybe, your last chance," she muttered and left the office.

Now I sat gazing at the bookcase, the pictures on her desk, the letters in frames congratulating her on her performance as an administrator in our upstate New York child welfare agency. Bored with the things decorating Mrs. McGuire's office, I turned around in my chair to stare out the windows. It was a sunny spring day. I sighed as I looked out at the trees, their shiny green leaves and budding blossoms calling to me. Everything was growing like weeds because of the heavy spring rain, and I could tell Philip, the grounds-keeper, wasn't very happy to be mowing the endless lawns so early in the season. His face was screwed up in a scowl and I could just imagine him grumbling about the grass coming up so fast this year, you could watch it grow. For a moment I drifted away in the monotonous sound of Philip's lawnmower and the dazzling sunlight streaming in through the windows. I forgot I was in Mrs. McGuire's office, forgot I was slouching with my eyes closed.

I tried to remember my real mother, but my earliest memories are of being in an orphanage. I was in one other beside this one, then I got transfered here when I was nearly seven. I'm almost thirteen now, but even I would admit that I look no more than nine, maybe ten. Because I couldn't remember my real mother, Tommy Turner said I was probably one of those babies that doctors make in a laboratory.

"I bet you were born in a test tube and that's why you're so small. Something went wrong with the experiment," he'd said as we left the dining hall last night. The other kids all thought he was very clever and laughed at his joke. Laughed at me.

"Janet's mother and father were test tubes," they taunted.

"No," Tommy said. "Her father was a syringe and her mother was a test tube."

"Who named her Janet then?" Margaret asked doubtfully.

Tommy had to think.

"That was the name of her lab technician, Janet Taylor, so they gave her that name," he answered, and from the look on their faces, I could tell the other kids believed him.

Last night, like every night, I had wished with all my heart that I knew something about my past, some fact, a name, anything that I could say to Tommy and the others to prove that once upon a time I did have a real Mommy and Daddy. I wasn't a dwarf or a test tube baby, I was . . . well, I was like a butterfly—destined to be beautiful and soar high above the earth, high above troubles and doubts, high above nasty little kids who made fun of other people just because they were smaller and weaker.

BUTTERFLY

It's just that I hadn't burst from my cocoon yet. I was still a shy little girl, curled up in my quiet, cozy world. I knew that someday I would have to break free, to be braver, speak louder, grow taller, but right now that seemed all too scary. The only way I knew how to keep the taunts and teasing of the other kids from bothering me was to stay in my own little cocoon—where it was warm and safe and no one could hurt me. But someday, someday I would soar. Like a beautiful butterfly, I would climb higher and higher, flying high above them all. I'd show them.

Someday.

One

"Janet!" I heard Mrs. McGuire hiss, and my eyes snapped open. Her face was filled with fury, her mouth twisted, her gray eyes wide and lit up like firecrackers. "Sit up," she whispered through her clenched teeth, and then she forced a smile and turned to the couple standing behind her. "Right this way, Mr. and Mrs. Delorice," she said in a much nicer tone of voice.

I took a deep breath and held it, my fluttering heart suddenly sounding like a kettle drum in my chest. Mrs. McGuire stepped behind me so that the Delorices could get a good look at me. Mr. Delorice was tall and thin with dark hair and sleepy eyes. Mrs. Delorice sat in a wheelchair and was pretty, with hair the color of a red sunset. She had diminutive facial features like my own, but even more perfectly proportioned. Her hair floated around her shoulders in soft undulating waves. There was nothing sickly or frail looking about her, despite her wheelchair. Her complexion was rich like peaches and cream, her lips the shade of fresh strawberries.

She wore a bright yellow dress, my favorite color, and a string of tiny pearls around her neck. She looked like every other potential mommy I had seen except for the wheelchair and the tiny little shoes she wore. Although I'd never seen ballet shoes before, I thought that was what they were. If she was in a wheelchair, why was she wearing ballet shoes? I wondered.

Mr. Delorice pushed her right up to me. I was too fascinated to move, much less speak. Why would a woman in a wheelchair want to adopt a child my age?

"Mr. and Mrs. Delorice, this is Janet Taylor. Janet, Mr. and Mrs. Delorice."

"Hello," I said, obviously not loud enough to please Mrs. McGuire. She gestured for me to stand and I scrambled out of the chair.

"Please, dear, call us Sanford and Celine," the pretty woman said. She held out her hand and I took it gingerly, surprised at how firmly she held her fingers around mine. For a moment we only looked at each other. Then I glanced up at Sanford Delorice.

He was looking down at me, his eyes opening a bit wider to reveal their mixture of brown and green. He had his hair cut very short, which made his skinny face look even longer and narrower. He was wearing a dark gray sports jacket with no tie and a pair of dark blue slacks. The upper two buttons on his white shirt were open. I thought it was to give his very prominent Adam's apple breathing space.

"She's perfect, Sanford, just perfect, isn't she?" Celine said, gazing at me.

"Yes, she is, dear," Sanford replied. He had his long fingers still wrapped tightly around the handles of the wheelchair as if he was attached or afraid to let go.

"Did she ever have any training in the arts?" Celine asked Mrs. McGuire. She didn't look at Mrs. McGuire when she asked. She didn't look away from me. Her eyes were fixed on my face, and although her staring was beginning to make me feel creepy, I was unable to look away.

"The arts?"

"Singing, dancing . . . ballet, perhaps?" she asked.

"Oh no, Mrs. Delorice. The children here are not that fortunate," Mrs. McGuire replied.

Celine turned back to me. Her eyes grew smaller, even more intensely fixed on me.

"Well, Janet will be. She'll be that fortunate," she predicted with certainty. She smiled softly. "How would you like to come live with Sanford and myself, Janet? You'll have your own room, and a very large and comfortable one, too. You'll attend a private school. We'll buy you an entirely new wardrobe, including new shoes. You'll have a separate area in your room for your schoolwork and you'll have your own bathroom. I'm sure you'll like our house. We live just outside of Albany with a yard as large, if not larger than you have here."

"That sounds wonderful," Mrs. McGuire said as if she were the one being offered the new home, but Mrs. Delorice didn't seem at all interested in what she said. Instead she stared at me and waited for my response.

"Janet?" Mrs. McGuire questioned when a long moment of silence had passed.

How could I ever refuse this, and yet when I looked up at Sanford and back at Celine, I couldn't help feeling little footsteps of trepidation tiptoeing across my heart. I pushed the shadowy faces out of my mind, glanced at Mrs. McGuire, and then nodded.

"I'd like that," I said, wishing I was as good as Mrs. McGuire at faking a smile.

"Good," Celine declared. She spun her chair around to face Mrs. McGuire. "How soon can she leave?"

"Well, we have some paperwork to do. However, knowing all that we already know about you and your husband, your impressive references, the social worker's report, et cetera, I suppose . . ."

"Can we take her with us today?" Celine demanded impatiently.

My heart skipped a beat. Today? That fast?

For once Mrs. McGuire was at a loss for words.

"I imagine that could be done," she finally replied.

"Good," she said. "Sanford, why don't you stay

with Mrs. McGuire and fill out whatever paper-work has to be filled out. Janet and I can go outside and get more acquainted in the mean-time," she said. It was supposed to be a sugges-tion, I guess, but it sounded like an order to me. I looked at Mr. Delorice and could see the muscles in his jaw were clenched, along with his fingers on the wheelchair handles.

"But there are documents that require both signatures," Mrs. McGuire insisted.

"Sanford has power of attorney when it comes to my signature," Celine countered. "Janet, can you push my chair? I don't weigh all that much," she added smiling.

I looked at Mrs. McGuire. She nodded and Sanford stepped back so that I could take hold of the handles.

"Where shall we go, Janet?" she asked me.

"I guess we can go out to the garden," I said uncertainly. Mrs. McGuire nodded again.

"That sounds wonderful. Don't be any longer than you have to, Sanford," she called back as I started to push her to the door. I went ahead and opened it and then I pushed her through.

I started down the hallway, overwhelmed and amazed with myself and what was happening. Not only was I going to have parents, but I had found a mother who wanted me to take care of her, almost as much as I wanted her to take care of me. What a strange and wonderful new beginning, I thought as I wheeled my new mother toward the sunny day that awaited us.

* * *

"Has it been difficult for you living here, Janet?" Celine asked after I had wheeled her outside. We followed the path to the garden.

"No, ma'am," I said, trying not to be distracted by the kids who were looking our way.

"Oh, don't call me ma'am, Janet. Please," she said, turning to place her hand over mine. It felt so warm. "Why don't you call me Mother. Let's not wait to get to know each other. Just do that immediately," she pleaded.

"Okay," I said. I could tell already that Mrs. Delorice didn't like to be argued with.

"You speak so softly, darling. I suppose you've felt so insignificant, but you won't feel that way anymore. You're going to be famous, Janet. You're going to be spectacular," she declared with such passion in her voice it made the breath catch in my throat.

"Me?"

"Yes, you, Janet. Come around and sit on this bench," she said when we had reached the first one along the pathway. She folded her hands in her lap and waited until I sat. Then she smiled. "You float, Janet. Do you realize that? You glide almost as if you're walking on a cloud of air. That's instinctive. Grace is something you're either born with or not, Janet. You can't learn it. No one can teach that to you.

"Once," she said as her green eyes darkened, "I had grace. I glided, too. But," she said quickly changing her expression and tone back to a happier, lighter one, "let's talk about you first. I've been watching you."

"When?" I said, recalling what Mrs. McGuire had told me.

"Oh, on and off for a little more than two weeks. Sanford and I came here at different times of the day. Usually we sat in our car and watched you and your unfortunate brothers and sisters at play. I even saw you at your school," she admitted.

My mouth widened with surprise. They had followed me to school? She laughed.

"When I first set eyes on you, I knew I had to have you. I knew you were the one, Janet. You remind me so much of myself when I was your age."

"I do?"

"Yes, and when Sanford and I went home, I would think about you and dream about you, and actually see you gliding down our staircase and through our home. I could even hear the music," she said, with a faraway look in her eyes.

"What music?" I asked, starting to think that Mrs. Delorice might be a little more than just bossy.

"Music you'll dance to, Janet. Oh," she said, leaning forward to reach for my hand, "there is so much to tell you and so much to do. I can't wait to start. That's why I wanted Sanford to cut right through all that silly bureaucratic paperwork and take us both home. Home," she repeated, her smile softening even more. "I suppose that's a foreign word to you, isn't it? You've never had a home. I know all about you," she added.

"What do you know?" I asked. Maybe she knew something about my real mommy and daddy.

"I know you were an orphan shortly after your birth and ever since. I know some very stupid people came to find children to adopt and passed you by. That's their loss and my gain," she followed with a thin, high-pitched laugh.

"What did you mean when you said music I would dance to?" I asked.

She released my hand and sat back. For a moment I didn't think she was going to answer. She stared off toward the woods. A sparrow landed near us and studied us with curiosity.

"After I picked you out, I observed you, auditioning you in my own mind," she explained. "I studied your walk, your gestures, and your posture to see if you were capable of being trained to become the dancer I was to be, the dancer I can no longer even dream to be. Beyond a doubt I am convinced you can. Would you like that? Would you like to be a famous dancer, Janet?"

"A famous dancer? I've never thought about it," I said honestly. "I do like to dance. I like music too," I added.

"Of course you do," she responded. "Someone with your natural grace and rhythm has to love music, and you'll love to dance, too. You'll love the power. You'll feel . . ." She closed her eyes and took a deep breath. When she opened her eyes I saw that they were filled with an eerie light. "You'll feel you can soar like a bird. When you're good, and you will be good, you will lose yourself in the music, Janet. It will carry you off, just as it did for me so many, many times before I became crippled."

"What happened to you?" I dared to ask. It was obvious that talking about dancing made her emotional, but the eerie look in her eyes made me nervous and I wanted her to do something besides stare at me so intently.

Mrs. Delorice lost her soft, dreamy smile and gazed back at the building before turning to me and replying.

"I was in a very bad car accident. Sanford lost control of our vehicle one night when we were returning from a party. He had a little too much to drink, although he'll never ever admit to that. He claimed he was blinded by the lights of a tractor-trailer truck. We went off the road and hit a tree. He was wearing his seat belt but I had forgotten to put mine on. The door opened and I was thrown from the car. My spine was very badly damaged. I almost died."

"I'm sorry," I said quickly.

Her face hardened, the lines deepening as shadows darkened her complexion.

"I'm past being sorry. I was sorry for years, but being sorry for yourself doesn't help one bit, Janet. Never indulge in self-pity. You become incapable of helping yourself. Oh," she said excited again, the light in her eyes returning, "I have so much to tell you, to teach you. It's going to be wonderful for both of us. Are you excited, too?"

"Yes," I said. I was, but everything was moving so fast and I couldn't help feeling nervous and a little bit scared.

She turned toward the building.

"Where is he? I never saw a man waste so much time. Oh, but you'll get to admire him for his compassion and sensitivity," she said. "There isn't anything he wouldn't do for me now, and now," she said with a wider smile, "there isn't anything he won't do for you.

"Think of it, Janet, think of it," she urged, "for the first time in your life, you will have two loving people who will care more about you than they will for themselves. Oh yes, it's true, dear, precious Janet. Look at me. Why should I worry about myself anymore? I'm a prisoner in this damaged body forever, and Sanford, Sanford lives to make me happy. So you see," she said with that tiny, thin laugh again, "if my happiness depends on your happiness, Sanford will cherish you as much as I will.

"You will be happy, Janet," she said with such firmness it frightened me. It was almost as if she was commanding me to be happy. "That," she said, "I promise you."

Sanford stepped out of the building.

"It's about time," she muttered. "Come, Janet, dear. Let us begin your new life. Let's think of this as your true birth. Okay? We'll even use this day as your birthday from now on. Why not? Yes? I like that idea. Don't you?" she declared with another thin laugh. "Today is your birthday!"

"Sanford," she called before I could reply. Actually, I didn't know what to say. My birthday had never been very special to me. He started toward us. "This day is more extraordinary than we imagined. It's Janet's birthday."

"It is?" he asked, looking confused. "But, I thought . . ."

"It is." She stamped her words in the air between them and he nodded.

She reached her hand out to me.

"Come along now," she said. "We're going home to celebrate."

When I saw the grim look on Sanford's face and remembered the crazy light that had come into Mrs. Delorice's eyes, I wondered just what had I gotten myself into.

Two

Despite the years I had lived at the orphanage, there wasn't anyone I was sorry to leave behind. My good-byes were quick. Those who had made fun of me for so long just stared with envy. No one had much to say. Only Margaret came up to me as I was getting my things together and whispered, "What kind of a mother is a mother in a wheelchair?"

"One who wants to love me," I replied and left her gnawing on the inside of her cheek.

Celine was already in the car, waiting. Sanford helped me with my things and then opened the car door for me as if he were my chauffeur. They had a very expensive-looking black car with leather seats that felt as soft as marshmallows. I thought the car was as big as a limousine. It had the scent of fresh roses.

"Look at her, Sanford," Celine said. "She's not

the least bit sorry to be leaving that place. Are you, dear?"

"No . . ." The following word seemed hard to form, so alien. My tongue tripped over itself. "Mother."

"Did you hear her, Sanford? Did you hear what she called me?"

"I did, honey." He looked back at me and smiled for the first time since I'd met him. "Welcome to our family, Janet."

"Thank you," I said, but I knew I had spoken too softly for either of them to hear.

"We had a nice conversation in the garden while you were crossing T's and dotting I's, Sanford."

"Oh?"

"Janet told me she loves to dance," Celine said.

"Really?" Sanford sounded surprised.

I had said I liked dancing, but I hadn't done enough dancing to say I loved it, especially the sort of dancing she meant. She turned to face me.

"I was younger than you when I started training, Janet. My mother was very supportive, maybe because her mother, my grandmother Annie, was a prima ballerina. It broke my mother's heart almost as much as it did mine when I had to stop." She had turned to look at me and I could see the strange light had returned to her eyes.

She took a deep breath before continuing.

"Both my parents are still alive. They live in Westchester in the same house where my brother Daniel and I were raised," she explained.

My heart began to pound again. It was one

thing to dream of having a mommy and daddy, but another to think up an entire family with grandparents and uncles and aunts. Maybe there was a cousin, too, a girl about my age with whom I could become best friends.

"Unfortunately, both of Sanford's parents are gone," she continued. She gazed at him again. "His sister Marlene lives in Denver but we don't see her very much. She doesn't approve of me."

"Celine, please," he said weakly.

"Yes, Sanford's right. No unpleasantness, never again. You don't need to know any of the unpleasantness I've had to bear. You've known enough during your poor little life," she said. "You don't have to worry about money, either. We're rich."

"You shouldn't say things like that, Celine," Sanford gently chastised. I could tell immediately that he was sorry he'd spoken.

"Why not? Why shouldn't I be proud? Sanford owns and operates a glass factory. We're not as big as Corning, but we're competition for them, aren't we, Sanford?" she bragged.

"Yes, dear." He looked back at me. "Once you've settled in, I'll show you the plant."

"You can show her, but she's not going to spend a great deal of time down there, Sanford. She'll be too busy with her schooling and her dancing," Celine assured him.

A cold drop of ice trickled along my spine.

"What if I can't be a dancer?" I asked. Would they send me back?

"Can't be? Don't be silly, Janet. I told you, you have grace. You already dance. You dance when you walk, the way you hold yourself, the way you look at people, the way you sit. Having been gifted with this myself, I know how to recognize it in someone else. You won't fail," she said confidently. "I won't let you fail. I'll be your cushion, your parachute. You won't suffer the sort of disappointments I suffered," she pledged.

Even more anxious, I squeezed my arms around myself. When I was younger, I would pretend my arms were my mother's arms, holding me. I would close my eyes and imagine the scent of her hair, the softness of her face, the warmth of her lips on my forehead. Would Celine ever hold me like that? Or would her being in a wheelchair make that too difficult to do?

I gazed out the window at the scenery that flowed by. It was as if the whole world had become liquid and ran past us in a stream of trees, houses, fields, and even people. Few took any special notice of us even though I felt so special. They should all be cheering as we go by. I'm not an orphan anymore.

"Looks like some rain ahead," Sanford predicted and nodded at a ridge of dark clouds creeping toward us from the horizon.

"Oh phooey," Celine declared. "I want the sun to shine all day today."

Sanford smiled and I could feel the tension ease out of him.

"I'll see what I can do," he said. The way he looked at her, doted on her, I had no doubt that if he could, he would shape the weather and the world to please her. There was love here, I thought, some sort of love. I only hoped it was the right sort.

When I finally set my eyes on their house, I thought I had fallen into a storybook. No one really lived in such a house, I thought, even as we went up the long circular driveway with perfectly trimmed hedges on both sides. Evenly spaced apart were charcoal gray lampposts, the bulbs encased in shiny brass fixtures. Celine hadn't been exaggerating. They did have more lawn than the orphanage. There were large sprawling red maple trees with leaves that looked like dark rubies, and a pair of enormous weeping willow trees, the tips of the branches touching the ground to form a cave of shadows. I could just make out the shape of two benches and a small fountain surrounded by the darkness. Squirrels scurried around the fountain and over the benches, up trees and through the grass with a nervous, happy energy. I saw a rabbit pop out from behind the trees, look our way, and then hop toward the taller grass.

I turned to look at the house, a tall two-story with a porch that wrapped all the way around. Two robins paraded over the four wooden front steps. Alongside them was a ramp for Celine's wheelchair and a sparrow stood so still on it, he looked stuffed.

It all seemed so magical, touched by a fairy's wand and brought to life.

"Home sweet home," Celine declared. "We did a lot to modernize it after we bought it. It's Victorian," she explained. I didn't know what that meant, but from the way she said it, I understood it was impressive.

The house looked like it had been recently painted, a bright, crisp white. The paired entry doors had mirrored glass in the top halves of each and all the windows on the first and second floors had filmy white curtains in them. Only the attic windows were dark, with what looked like dark gray drapes pulled closed.

"Your room faces the east so you will have bright morning sunshine to wake you every day," Celine explained.

To the right and just behind the house was the garage, but Sanford stopped the car in front and got out quickly. He opened the trunk, took out Celine's wheelchair, and moved to open her door.

"Get her things," Celine commanded as soon as she was in her chair.

"Don't you want me to get you into the house first?"

"No. I asked you to get her things," she repeated firmly. "Where is that Mildred?" she muttered under her breath.

I stepped out and stared up at the house, my new home. Celine had gotten a little of her wish. The clouds had parted briefly and rays of light made the windows glitter as we stood there, but before we went up to the front doors, the clouds shifted and deepened the shadows again. Celine shuddered and tightened the shawl Sanford had placed around her shoulders.

"How do you like it?" she asked me expectantly.

"It's beautiful," I said.

However, most of my life homes with families in them looked beautiful to me, even if they were half the size and cost of this one. Behind closed doors and on the other side of curtains, families sat having dinner or watching television together. Brothers and sisters teased each other, but told each other secret things and held each other's dreams in strict confidence. There were shoulders to lean on, lips that would kiss away tears, voices that would warm cold and frightened little hearts. There were daddies who had strong arms to hold you, daddies who smelled of the outdoors and aftershave, daddies with love in their smiles; and mommies who were beautiful and soft, who were scented with flowery aromas, perfumes that filled your nostrils and stirred your imagination and filled your head with dreams of becoming as lovely and as pretty.

Yes, it was a beautiful house. They were all beautiful houses.

"Hurry along, please, Sanford," Celine said, wheeling herself to the base of the ramp.

He struggled with two suitcases and one of the smaller bags. I started toward her chair, but she turned in anticipation. It was as if she had eyes behind her head.

"No, Janet. I don't want you doing anything this strenuous. You can't afford to pull a tendon."

I stopped, confused. Pull a tendon? I had no idea what she meant.

"It's all right," Sanford told me and somehow managed to take hold of the chair as he kept the suitcases under his arm. He pushed her up the ramp and I followed. When we reached the porch, he put down the suitcases and hurried around to unlock the door.

"Where is that fool?" she asked him sharply. I had no idea who she was talking about. Did someone else live in their beautiful house?

"It's all right," he said inserting his door key.

Celine turned and smiled at me.

"Now you can push me, sweetheart," she said, and I moved quickly to the back of the chair.

Sanford opened the door and we entered the house. The entryway was wide with mirrors on both sides. On the right was a coatrack and a small table on which were some sort of pamphlets. When I looked closer, I saw they were programs for a dance recital. On the front of one was Celine's picture. Above it in big red letters were the words *Sleeping Beauty*.

"I want you to see the studio first," she said when she saw what had captured my attention. "Sanford, bring her things upstairs to her room and see if you can find Mildred. We'll be along in a few minutes."

I saw there was a special elevator chair that ran up the side of the stairway. At the top was another wheelchair. Celine wheeled herself deeper into the house and I followed slowly, drinking everything in: the beautiful paintings on the walls, all of dancers, one who looked very much like Celine.

"This is our living room," she said, nodding at a room on the left.

I could only glance at it because she moved

quickly down the hall. I saw the fancy pink and white sofa with frills along the base, a red cushioned chair, the fieldstone fireplace and mantel, above which was a grand painting of Celine in a ballet costume.

"Here," she declared, pausing at another doorway.

I stepped up beside her and looked into the room. It was large and empty, with a shiny wooden floor. All around the room were full-length mirrors and on one side was a long wooden bar.

"This is my studio and now it is yours," she declared. "I had a wall knocked out and two rooms connected. You can spare no expense when it comes to your art."

"Mine?" I asked.

"Of course, Janet. I will get you the best instructor, Madame Malisorf, who has trained some very famous Russian ballet dancers and once was an accomplished ballerina herself. She was my teacher and mentor." And again that faraway, eerie look came over her.

"I really don't know anything about ballet," I said, my voice trembling. I was afraid she would want to return me to the orphanage immediately when she learned how clumsy I was.

"That's all right. That's good. I'd rather you didn't know anything," she replied, taking my hand.

"You would?"

"Yes. This way you're pure, an innocent, an untouched dancer, not contaminated by any mediocre teacher. Madame Malisorf will be pleased," she assured me. "She loves working with pure talent."

"But I don't have any talent," I said.

"Of course you do."

"I don't think I've even seen a ballet on television," I confessed.

She laughed and I was glad to see her normal face returning.

"No, I don't imagine you did, living in those places with children who have had no opportunities. You mustn't be so afraid," she said softly, squeezing my hand. "Ballet is not as difficult as you might imagine and it's not some strange form of dance reserved only for the very rich. It's just another way of telling a story, a beautiful way, through dance. Ballet is the foundation of all Western theatrical dance. People who want to be modern dancers or dancers in show business are always advised to start with ballet."

"Really?"

"Of course." She smiled. "So you see, you will be doing something that will help you in so many ways. You'll have wonderful posture, more grace, rhythm, and beauty. You will be my prima ballerina, Janet."

She stared at me with her eyes so full of hope and love I could only smile back. Suddenly we heard a door slam and someone hurrying down the stairs. She turned her chair and I looked back to see a tall young blond girl come down the hallway. She was dressed in a maid's uniform. She had large brown eyes with a nose a little too long and a mouth a little too wide with a weak, bony chin.

"I'm sorry, Mrs. Delorice. I didn't hear you drive up."

"Probably because you had those stupid earphones in your ears again, listening to that ugly rock music," Celine quipped.

The maid cringed and began to shake her head vigorously.

"Stop sniveling, Mildred, and meet our daughter, Janet," Celine said sharply and then her voice softened. "And Janet, this is our maid, Mildred Stemple."

"How do you do," Mildred said with a small dip. When she smiled, her features shifted and she actually looked pretty. "Call me Milly."

"She will not," Celine corrected quickly. "Her name is Mildred," she told me firmly.

Mildred's smile wilted.

"Hello . . . Mildred," I said, not wanting to make waves.

"I was making sure her room was clean and ready, Mrs. Delorice," Mildred said, continuing her explanation for not coming to the front door.

"You're always leaving things for the last minute, Mildred. I don't know why I keep you. We'll have an early dinner tonight. You have the turkey roasting, I assume?"

"Oh yes, Mrs. Delorice."

"Well, see to getting the rest ready," Celine ordered.

Mildred glanced at me, smiled quickly, and left.

"That," Celine said, raising her eyes to the

ceiling, "is my act of charity. Anyway, back to what I was saying. Madame Malisorf will be here the day after tomorrow to meet you."

"The day after tomorrow?"

"We don't want to waste time, dear. In dance, especially ballet, training is so important. I wish I had found you when you were years younger. It would have been easier, but don't fret about it. You're at a perfect age. You'll begin with a sequence of exercises to build up your precious little muscles. There is always a great deal of stretching and warming up to prevent injury. You'll learn how to use the barre."

"Barre?"

"The bar there is known as a *barre*," she said and spelled it out. "All the terms in ballet are French. Ballet began in France. You use the barre to steady yourself during the first part of ballet class. It provides resistance when you press down on it and helps to lengthen the spine." She laughed. "Think of it as your first partner. I used to give my barre a name. I called it Pierre," she said with a perfect French pronunciation. "I'm sure you'll find a suitable name for your first partner, too."

I gazed through the doorway at the barre, wondering how I could ever think of it as a person.

"Come along, dear. We have so much to do. I need to have you fitted for pointe shoes and buy you leotards first thing in the morning."

"What about school?" I asked. She kept wheeling and then paused at the foot of the stairway.

"Don't worry. I'm enrolling you in a private school. We can do that later. First things first," she said. She started to move into the chairlift.

First things first? But wouldn't my schooling be the first thing?

"Let me help you, darling," Sanford called as he came down the stairs.

"I'm fine," she said slipping into the lift chair. She pressed a button and it began to move up the railing. I watched her for a moment. She looked radiant and excited as she rose above us.

"How wonderful," Sanford declared at my side. "Just your coming here has already filled her with new strength. We're blessed to have you, my dear."

I gazed up at him and wondered what I had done to bring such happiness to two people who only hours ago had been complete strangers. I couldn't help being afraid that they had mistaken me for someone else.

Three

When I stood in the doorway of the room that was to be my very own, I felt my mouth fall open. Never in any of my most wonderful fantasies could I have imagined a room as beautiful as this, or as big as this, or as warm and cozy. And this was the first time in my life that a room was all mine, too!

"How do you like it?" Celine asked excitely.

For a moment I couldn't speak. Like it? *Like* is too weak a word, I thought. I was to sleep here? To live and do my schoolwork here?

"It's so big," I began. I was afraid to step inside, afraid that if I did, it would all pop and disappear like a nice dream. Celine wheeled herself forward and Sanford stood behind me with his hands on my shoulders while she inspected the room to be sure Mildred had done a good job.

"Good. At least your things have been put

away," she said. "We're going shopping first thing in the morning to get you some decent clothes," she added.

"I'd like to check on the factory first, dear. I'll come right back and . . ." Sanford began meekly.

"You can stay away from your precious factory one more day, Sanford. Your manager is quite competent. Anyway," she said, gazing at me, "what's more important?" She looked at him pointedly. He said nothing.

Anxious to avoid their heated words and glances, I entered my room. The curtains were flamingo pink as were the canopy, pillows, and comforter on the four-pillar bed. There was an eggshell white desk with a lamp that had a base shaped like a duck. On the walls were paintings of ballet dancers.

"Those are scenes from famous ballets, Janet," Celine explained. "That's *Swan Lake,* and that's *Le Jeune Homme et la Mort.* That one is *Romeo and Juliet,"* she said, nodding at the one over the bed. "I want you to be surrounded in dance— sleep, eat, and drink it just the way I did. In time it's all you'll care about," she said, and again I felt it was an order.

She wheeled herself to a cabinet next to the closet and opened it.

"Here you'll find tapes and CDs of music I want you to listen to and get to know so well you can hum entire productions. The music must become a part of you. You'll surely do as I did, hear the music, even while you're away from the studio, and you'll find yourself wanting to pirouette or perform a *changement de pieds.*"

"What's that?"

She looked at Sanford and smiled.

"Frequently you need to change the position of your feet, from right foot in front to left foot in front or vice versa. That's a jump in which you land with the other foot in front. So, changement de pieds, change of the feet. Don't worry. It will be easier than you think, especially for you," she said.

I looked at Sanford to see if he had as much confidence in me. His eyes were filled with smiles.

"Let her look around at her new room, Celine."

"Of course," she said, backing away. "Your bathroom is through that door."

I peered in at the round bathtub and stall shower. All of the fixtures were shiny brass, and then I saw the towels on the racks. There was something written on them. I drew closer to read.

"My name is on the towel!" I exclaimed.

Sanford laughed.

"And on the glass and the little soap dish," he added.

Amazed, I took it all in.

"But how did you do all this so fast?"

"Remember, I have a factory, and connections," he said, clearly amused at my question.

"But how did you know I would come here to live?" I pursued.

He gazed at Celine, who had wheeled up to the bathroom door.

"I told you, dear, from the moment I set eyes on you, I knew you were the one. The only one. We were destined to be a family."

I thought I would simply explode from the way happiness filled my heart. A beautiful bed, furniture, personalized bathroom items, new clothes, everything I could ever want. It was Christmas in springtime.

"Are you happy?" Sanford asked.

"Oh yes." I practically shouted the words and thought, finally, I'm speaking loudly enough to please even Mrs. McGuire.

"Good. Change into something casual and I'll show you our grounds," Sanford told me. "There's a lake out back, and in the summer we get geese."

"I'm going to call Madame Malisorf," Celine said, "and confirm your first lesson for the day after tomorrow. I'm so excited—I wonder if we should change it to first thing tomorrow? No, tomorrow we'll have to get your pointe shoes and leotards. We mustn't get ahead of ourselves."

"Shouldn't you wait before buying her the pointe shoes, dear?" Sanford asked softly.

"Absolutely not." She turned to me. "She's going to be Madame Malisorf's best student. Since me, of course. What a wonderful day!" She reached for me and then for Sanford. "We're finally a family," she said, looking at us with that faraway gaze.

I thought the tears that were burning under my eyelids would go streaming down my cheeks, but they remained where they were to wait for another time.

After I changed into a pair of old jeans and put on a blouse and sneakers, I wandered along the upstairs hallway. There was another bedroom with the door shut tight and then Sanford and Celine's room. Celine was inside, resting in bed and speaking to Sanford. I didn't want to seem like I was spying on them, so I turned to go downstairs and wait, when I heard Celine mention my name.

"Janet will blossom like a flower in our soil, won't she, Sanford?"

"Yes, dear," he said. "Please. Just rest a bit now. It's been a very long and emotional day for all of us."

"And when she does," Celine continued, ignoring him, "she will dazzle audiences the way I was meant to dazzle them."

Dazzle audiences? I thought. Me? The one the other children called Miss Fraidy Cat for as long as I could remember? The one who couldn't speak loud enough for someone right beside me to hear properly? Perform before audiences and dazzle them? How could I? As soon as Celine and Sanford realized I couldn't, they would send me back. I was so sure of it, my heart shriveled into a tight little knot. The beautiful room, this home, the promise of a family, all of it really was just a dream. I bowed my head and slowly descended the stairs.

I wandered into the living room and gazed up at

the painting of Celine that hung above the mantel. The artist had captured her in the middle of a leap, maybe that changement de pieds she had described. Her legs, the ones that were hidden under a blanket, lifeless and limp now, looked shapely and muscular in the painting. She resembled a bird, soaring, just as she had described how I would feel someday. How graceful and beautiful she looked against the dark background. The painting was so lifelike, I half expected her to land before me.

"So here you are." I turned to see Sanford in the doorway. "Celine's taking a little rest. Come on. I'll show you our grounds. We'll walk down to the lake," he added and I noticed that he spoke in an entirely different voice when Celine wasn't around.

When we got outside I saw that the sky had cleared as Celine had said it would. I was beginning to wonder if everyone and everything did as Celine asked.

"This way," Sanford said, turning right at the bottom of the steps. He walked with his hands behind his back, his tall, lean body leaning forward. He took long, lanky strides, one for every two of mine. "This house was a find. It was in very good shape for its age, but we made a number of changes and improvements," he said. "I'm sure you will be as happy here as we have been, Janet." He smiled at me and nodded at the descending hillside before us. "Just over the crest is our lake. I have a rowboat, but we haven't used it for some time. Can you swim?"

"No sir," I said softly, afraid to add another "can't" to my name. Can't dance. Can't swim. Can't stay.

"Oh, well, that will have to be remedied before summer, and please, don't call me sir. If you can't call me Dad yet, just call me Sanford, okay?" His eyes twinkled and I relaxed and smiled back at him. Somehow I'd already gotten the impression that Sanford was going to be a lot easier to please than Celine.

We walked on.

"I have a service that comes twice a week to care for the grounds," he said. He waved his long arm toward the east. "We own all this property and then some. I've left woods intact so we have the privacy and the feeling we're out in nature. We're really not that far from the city. The private school you'll attend is only fifteen miles away, actually. Celine has already made all the arrangements. I just have to bring you there to enroll you."

"She has?" It made me feel strange to think that Celine had been planning a life for me, for us, before I'd even met her. What if I had said no to going home with them? But then, I was an orphan, and orphans never say no.

Sanford laughed at the perplexed look on my face.

"Oh yes. Celine has been preparing for your arrival literally from the first moment she set eyes on you, Janet. I'll never forget that day. She was so excited, she couldn't sleep and she wouldn't stop talking about you. She talked late into the night and when I woke up the next morning, your name was the first word on her lips."

Rather than fill me with joy, these words sent tiny electric shocks of fear along my spine. What did Celine see in me that I couldn't see in myself, that no one had ever seen before? What if it was all untrue?

"How come you don't have any children of your own?" I asked.

For a few minutes he walked along silently, and I thought perhaps he hadn't heard me, but then he paused, looked back at the house, and sighed. The grim expression that I had seen earlier was quickly returning to his face.

"I wanted to have children. From the first day we were married, I planned on having a family, but Celine was too devoted to her career, and she believed giving birth would take away from her power as a dancer.

"Anyway," he said, continuing to walk toward the hill, "she would be the first to admit she didn't have the temperament for children in those days." He shook his head. "You would have had to look far and wide to find someone as moody. I felt like an inept weatherman, unable to predict the days of sunshine or the days of gloom. One moment she was laughing, light, and happy, and the next, because of some dissatisfaction with her rehearsal, she would become dark and sad, wilting like a flower without water. Nothing I did could cheer her. But," he said, smiling at me again, "now that you're here, that's all going to change. There'll be no more dark days."

How could I make Celine so happy that she'd forget about her legs? Would watching me dance really make her feel any better about never being able to dance herself? How was I to be responsible for Celine's happiness? I was too small and too shy. I'd never be able to do it.

"I used to feel like I was walking barefoot on shattered glass when I returned home from business every day," Sanford continued and his voice interrupted my worrying. It was nice listening to him, to hear him open his heart to me as if I was already part of his family or had been a part of it for years. I just wish the thoughts and desires he confided in me were pleasant ones, but the more Sanford spoke the more I realized how sad and bitter he was. "Celine's moods were totally unpredictable, and after the accident they got worse. Now, that's all going to be different," he emphasized cheerily. I could tell he was trying not to say anything else gloomy.

We stopped at the top of the hill and looked out at the lake. It shimmered in the sunlight, the water looking smooth as ice. There was a dock just below us with the rowboat he had described.

"The lake's not that big, only about a half a mile or so, but it's nice to have water on your property. And the geese who visit every year are quite a sight toward the end of the summer. You'll see," he said. I was happy to hear him plan on my being here for a long time.

"It's pretty," I said. I was thankful he'd changed the subject.

"Yes, it is." He thought a moment and then

looked at me. "Well, I've been talking about us so much, I haven't given you a chance to talk about yourself. What are the things you like to do? Did you ever ice-skate or roller-skate?" he asked.

I shook my head.

"I'm sure you haven't ever gone skiing. Do you play any sports?"

"I only play sports in school. I usually don't play at the orphanage."

"What about books? Do you like to read?"

"Yes."

"Good. We have a very good library. I like to read. I suppose you like television."

I nodded.

"And movies?"

"I haven't gone many times," I said. Actually, I could count the times on my fingers.

"Your life is going to change so much, Janet. I'm almost more excited for you than I am for us. Come along," he added after a moment. "I'll show you the wild berry bushes."

I hurried to keep up with him. Berry bushes, a lake with a rowboat, beautiful flowers and personal gardeners, a private school, and new clothes. I was beginning to believe I really was Cinderella! I just hoped that I could hold off the stroke of midnight for as long as possible.

That night I had my first dinner in my new home. Celine wore a candy apple red knit dress with gold teardrop earrings and a necklace that had a cameo in a gold frame. She looked beautiful. Sanford wore a suit and tie. I had only the worn-out light blue dress I had worn at the orphanage for our first meeting.

The dining room was lit by a large chandelier over the table. All of the dishes, the napkins, candles, and silverware looked so expensive I was afraid to touch a thing. Sanford sat at one end of the long table and Celine at the other with me on the side. Mildred began to serve the food just moments after we sat down. Nothing felt as strange as having a servant. From the day we were able to do for ourselves at the orphanage, we took care of our own needs.

I watched how Celine ate, pecking at her food like a small bird. Meanwhile Sanford explained to me which piece of silverware to use and dining etiquette. Everything was so delicious and I was very hungry, but Celine didn't allow me to eat as much as I would have liked.

"Don't offer her seconds on the potatoes," she commanded when Sanford reached for the bowl. "From this day forward, she has to watch her diet. Dancers," she explained, turning to me, "have to maintain their figures. Excess fat just won't do. It will slow you down and make you clumsy. Even though I don't dance anymore, I still watch my figure. Habits become part of who you are, define your personality. Remember that, Janet. I'm passing all my wisdom on to you, the wisdom that was passed on to me by very famous and successful people."

I left the table that night still feeling a little hungry, something I never did at the orphanage. How strange it was to look at all those delicious things and have to keep from tasting them. I glanced at Celine every time Sanford passed something along, and if she frowned or looked displeased, I didn't take any of it. Passing on the delicious-looking chocolate cake with creamy white frosting made my stomach grumble loudest.

"You'll notice," Celine said, wheeling beside me as we went to the living room, "that you don't have a television set in your room. I know teenagers are fond of that, but between your schoolwork and your dancing, you won't have time for much else, especially frivolous things. I never did."

"I didn't watch a lot of television at the orphanage," I replied. "There was only the one set in the recreational room and the older boys always decided what we would all see. I'd rather read."

"Good. I have a book on ballet that I want you to start tonight," she told me and wheeled past me into the living room. I followed and watched her pluck a book from the shelves. She held it out for me and I hurried to take it.

"It's full of basic information," she said, "so you won't look stupid when you meet Madame Malisorf the day after tomorrow."

"Oh, she's far too excited to read and retain all that, Celine," Sanford said quietly. I couldn't help but think that if he just spoke more strongly, Celine might just listen to him.

"Nonsense. I'm sure she's tired, too, and she'll want to go up to her room, get into her bed, and read." She turned to me, obviously looking for my agreement.

I looked at Sanford, at the book, and then at Celine.

"Yes," I said. "I am tired."

"Of course. It's not every day that you get to start your life over again," Celine said. She reached up for my hand and held it. "We're so alike, you and I, it's as if you really were my daughter."

I saw tears in her eyes. They put tears into mine. My heart thumped with the promise of finding real love, real joy.

"Get a good night's rest," she said. "Welcome to your new home."

She pulled me down to her and kissed me on the cheek. It was the first time in my life someone who wanted to be my mother had kissed me. I swallowed back my tears of happiness and headed out the door. Sanford stopped me and kissed me on the cheek, too.

"Good night, Janet. Just call me if you need anything," he said.

I thanked him and hurried up the stairway with the ballet book in my hands.

Then I went into my room and just stood there gazing around in wonderment.

I had a home.

I was someone's child.

Finally.

Four

Celine was so excited about getting me ready for my ballet lessons the next day that she was up and at my door before I had opened my eyes. When I had finally laid my head on the fluffy pillow last night, I had turned and gazed at myself in the wall mirror. The bed was so large, I looked even smaller than I was. It made me laugh. But it was so comfortable, the most comfortable bed I had ever slept in, and all the linen smelled fresh and brand new. The next thing I knew, it was morning.

"Rise and shine, rise and shine," Celine sang as she wheeled herself into my room. "We have a great deal to do today, Janet."

I rubbed the sleep out of my eyes and sat up.

"Oh, you slept in your underwear!" she cried. "Don't you have a nightie?"

"No," I said.

"How do they send you out into the world without a nightie? Up, up, up. Get washed and dressed and come down to breakfast in fifteen minutes. We're off to the shops," she said with a sweep of her hand. Then she turned and wheeled out of my room.

I hurried to do what she asked, and in ten minutes, I was on my way down the stairs. Sanford was already dressed in his jacket and tie and sitting at the breakfast table reading the newspaper.

"Mildred," Celine called as soon as I set foot in the dining room.

Mildred came from the kitchen carrying a tray with orange juice, buttered toast, and a poached egg. I had never had a poached egg before. I stared at it all when it was set before me.

"You start your diet today," Celine explained when she saw my curious expression.

"Diet?" I had never been accused of being overweight. Everyone always thought I was under-developed. "But I don't weigh a lot," I said.

Celine laughed.

"Diet isn't something you watch just to lose weight. Diet in this case means eating properly. A dancer is an athlete and has to eat and live like one, Janet," Celine explained. "Go on, eat," she ordered.

Sanford lowered his paper and gave me a sympathetic smile as I drank my juice.

"Did you sleep well?" he asked.

"Yes," I said.

Celine leaned toward me to whisper, "Daddy."

47

"Yes, Daddy," I corrected.

"Good," Sanford said. "Good." He returned to his paper while Celine went on about our schedule.

"I have appointments arranged at the shoe store for your pointe shoes, and then we'll go to the shop where I will get you your dancing outfits. After that we'll go to the department store and get you some more clothes, regular shoes, undergarments, and a nice jacket for you to wear," she cataloged. "Oh, and a nightie."

"What about school?" I asked between bites. I couldn't help thinking about what it was going to be like to have new teachers and meet new children my age.

"School can wait another day," she declared. "I'm sure you're a very good student and it won't take you very long to catch up."

I was a good student, but I was still surprised at how confident she was about my abilities. Sanford folded his paper, sipped his coffee, and nodded.

"After that, we'll swing by the factory," he added.

"If we have time," Celine corrected.

I had barely swallowed my last bite of breakfast when she pushed away from the table and declared I should go brush my teeth and "Do your bathroom business." We were to meet at the front door in ten minutes.

Everything was ten minutes, five minutes. For a woman in a wheelchair, she had an unbelievable amount of energy. Rushing up the stairs, I thought I had been woken to participate in some sort of marathon, but I was afraid to utter a single syllable of complaint. Sanford seemed very happy about Celine's excitement and energy and they wanted to do so much for me.

By the time I returned, Celine was already in the car waiting. Sanford was just putting her wheelchair in the trunk.

"Hurry," she called. "I want to get everything done in one day."

I ran to the car and got in. Moments later, we were off.

"Getting the proper pointe shoes is paramount to success as a dancer," Celine lectured as we drove along. "In ballet, maybe more than in anything, initial preparations are very, very important. Your shoes should fit like a second skin. There is no room for growth. When you put them on before practice, don't tie the drawstring too tight. You can damage your Achilles tendon. Let me see your feet," she suddenly ordered.

"My feet?"

"Yes, yes, your feet. I need to check something. I should have done it before," she muttered.

I took off my sneakers and peeled off my socks. She reached back between the seats and pulled my feet toward her and inspected my toes.

"Oh," she cried, "these toenails are too long. Didn't they teach you anything at that orphanage? You must keep your toenails short. Cut them every morning, every morning, do you hear?"

"Yes," I said, nodding.

She reached into her purse and found a nail clipper. She handed it to me and watched as I trimmed my toenails. My hands shook and I thought I might cut myself, but Celine was starting to sound angry and I wanted to please her.

"Are you sure the store will be open this early, Celine?" Sanford asked as we approached the business district.

"Of course I'm sure. I made a specific appointment. They know how important this is to me," she added, and her voice was finally calming.

I put on my socks and sneakers quickly and gazed out the window as we slowed down and stopped before the specialty shop. Sanford hurried around to get Celine's wheelchair out of the trunk.

"It's such an inconvenience having to wait for that damn thing, and Sanford moves slower than a turtle," she muttered. She was so anxious to get into the store and have me fitted with pointe shoes. I wished I could be as excited about it as she was, but I felt as if I had been caught up in a whirlwind and barely had a chance to breathe. As soon as she was in her chair, she called to me. "Come on, Janet. We're late."

When we entered the store, the salesman, a short, chubby bald man with thin wire bifocals planted on his thick nose, came waddling from the rear to greet us.

"Mrs. Delorice," he said. "Good morning. It's so nice to see—"

"Here she is," Celine interrupted. "Janet, sit and take off your sneakers and socks."

The salesman nodded at Sanford.

"Mr. Delorice."

"Good morning, Charles. How have you been?" Sanford asked.

"Oh, fine, just fine."

"Please, let's concentrate," Celine demanded.

Charles frowned and squatted to study my feet. He held them in his hands as if they were jewels, gently turning them from side to side. He felt around under my toes and pressed on my heels.

"Exquisite," he said.

"She may look small to you, but she is not fragile," Celine assured him.

"Oh, I can see the potential, Mrs. Delorice, yes. Let me get her fitted." He looked genuinely pleased.

He rose and headed back to the rear of the store.

"All pointe shoes are handmade," Celine explained. "There is no right or left to them, so don't be confused."

"They must cost a lot," I said. I hoped her money wouldn't be wasted.

"Of course they do if they're good ones, and you must have the best. Our equipment, our dress, all of our preparations are very important for us, Janet," she said. It was the first time she had included herself and it sounded funny. It was as if she would rise out of the wheelchair and do one of her pirouettes in the shoe store.

Charles brought three pairs and tried each on my feet. Celine tested them as much as he did. She had me stand and then walk across the store.

"Very graceful young lady," Charles commented. I was beginning to wonder if Celine was right. Maybe I could be a dancer.

"Yes, she is," Celine said, her eyes shining with excitement. "How do those feel, Janet? Remember, I want you to think of them as a second skin."

"Good, I guess," I said. I really wasn't sure. I had never worn this kind of shoe before, and I didn't know how they should feel.

"Those have Toe-Flo," Charles remarked, "the best stuff ever invented for padding."

"I don't want her to become too dependent on that. I want her feet to toughen quickly." Celine's eyes darkened.

"Oh, they will," he promised.

"We'll see. We'll take them," she concluded.

"Very good choice, Mrs. Delorice," Charles said and I could almost see the dollar signs floating through his mind.

I sat and began to take the shoes off.

"We have to have the best so we can develop quickly," Celine said. She smiled at me and stroked my hair. "We're going to become prima ballerinas."

I looked at Sanford, who stood near the doorway. Again, I caught him wearing an expression of very deep concern, his eyes dark and concentrated on Celine. Then he saw me gazing at him and he smiled quickly.

After the shoes were purchased, we went to a store that sold the dancing costumes, called tutus, and leotards. Celine bought me a half dozen outfits, and this was only the beginning of what soon became a shopping frenzy. We went to the department store and flew through the lingerie department, shoe department, and then the clothing department. The registers clicked and dinged, printing out reels of receipts. It was as if all the clothing I should have had since birth was being bought now. In one day I was catching up with children who hadn't been orphans. I barely had time to take a breath before I was being herded into another section of the store, measured, fitted, and dressed to model whatever Celine thought might look nice. Price tags didn't seem to matter. She never looked at a single one, nor did she blink an eye when the totals were rung up. All she did was hold her hand out to Sanford, who produced his credit card.

Just a day before, I had thought of myself as an object of charity, cast off, living as a child of the state, without parents, without family, without anyone really caring if I looked nice or felt comfortable in my clothing and shoes. Suddenly, I was a little princess. Who could blame me for being afraid that I would blink and be back at the orphanage, waking from a dream?

Almost as if it pained her, Celine reluctantly agreed to stop for lunch. Sanford took us to a nice restaurant and told me I could order whatever I wanted from the menu, but Celine intercepted immediately and forbade me from ordering a big juicy hamburger.

"Choose a salad," she said. "You have to watch your fat content now."

"She's growing," Sanford said softly. "She'll burn off any calories, Celine."

"It's not what she'll burn off that's important. It's development of good habits, Sanford. Please. I know what I'm doing. I was the one who trained, not you. And I don't want to hear about you spoiling her when I'm not with you, Sanford," she said, warning him with her eyes wide.

He looked at me and laughed, but it was a weak laugh, a laugh of embarrassment.

"I like salads," I said to stop any more arguments.

"There, you see. She has a natural proclivity to do the right thing. It's in her nature. She's instinctive, just as I was, Sanford. She's me. She understands," she said, smiling at me. As much as it made me uncomfortable, I knew I could easily please her. I just had to agree to go along with anything she said. I think I was beginning to understand why Sanford looked so grim all the time.

Sanford wanted us to share dessert, but Celine refused.

"She can have something after dinner tonight," she compromised and we were off again, this time to buy toiletries Celine decided I would need.

"I want you to take special care of your hair, Janet. Your complexion, your looks are very important. You're a performer, an artist, a living, natural work of art yourself. That's how I was

54

taught to think and believe and that's how I want you to think," she declared.

When we were in that section of the store, she pulled me aside so Sanford wasn't able to hear us.

"Have you had your period yet?" she asked.

"No," I answered softly. It embarrassed me to admit it because all the girls I knew who were my age and even some a year younger had already had their first period.

Celine looked intently at me a moment. Then she nodded.

"Nevertheless, we'll be prepared for it," she said, and bought what I would need.

By the time we left the business district and headed for Sanford's glass factory, I was getting tired. Celine, however, continued to look energized. She talked and talked about my ballet lessons, preparing me for my first session with Madame Malisorf.

"A ballet class is a carefully graded sequence of exercises lasting at least an hour and a half, Janet. You'll begin with stretching and warming-up exercises using the barre. Madame Malisorf likes to spend nearly an hour doing that. Next, you'll move to the center of the studio to work without support. This second part of the class we call *adage.* It consists of slow work emphasizing sustaining positions and balance. The third part of the class is called *allegro,* and that consists of fast work, combinations, sequences of steps with the big jumps and turns that make ballet impressive. Can you remember all that, Janet? Madame Malisorf will be happy if you do." It was clear from her tone of voice that I should memorize what she'd said.

I told her I had read some of it in the book she had given me and that I would be sure to mention it to Madame Malisorf.

"Good. You'll pick it up faster than anyone expects. I just know you will," she said.

"We're here," Sanford announced proudly. It seemed that aside from pleasing Celine, the factory was the most important thing in Sanford's life. Maybe soon I would be added to the list.

The factory looked much bigger than I had expected and there were dozens and dozens of cars parked in the lot. Sanford owned all this? No wonder money didn't seem to matter, I thought.

"I'm really very tired, Sanford," Celine suddenly said. "I should take a rest."

"But . . . well, can't I show Janet the plant and check on some matters?" The smile and proud glow were gone from his face.

"Take me home first," she commanded tersely. "Besides, Janet's seen the factory. Why does she have to go in and be exposed to all that dust?"

"Dust? It's not dusty inside, Celine. You know how proud I am of our industrial environment." He was starting to whine.

"Please," she groaned. "Between you and Daddy, I hear more than enough about business. My parents own a printing plant," she explained. "Please, drive on, Sanford."

I could see his jaw tightening as he looked at her and then he gazed at his factory and shrugged.

"I just thought since we were already here . . ." He had already given up. He sounded like one of us orphans when we'd been passed up by yet another set of potential parents.

"She's not just visiting us, Sanford. She's come to live with us. There will be other times," Celine reminded him.

"Of course. You're right, dear. Home it is," he said and started off with a sigh.

But what about my school? I couldn't help but wonder. Shouldn't we go there now?

Celine seemed to read my thoughts.

"In the morning Sanford will take you to the private school and have you enrolled," she said. "And when you come home, Madame Malisorf will be there, waiting for you.

"Then," she added, her face filled with that eerie light and excitement from before, "we'll begin again."

Five

Later that evening when Celine began to question me about what I had read in the book on ballet, I felt as if I had already enrolled in a new school. She was like a teacher, correcting, explaining, and assigning me more reading. She wanted to be sure I knew the names of all the famous ballets.

"I haven't told Madame Malisorf anything about your background, Janet. She doesn't have to know you've lived all your life in an orphanage," she said. "You could be a distant relative whom I've adopted."

It was the first time she had said anything that made me feel ashamed of where I'd come from. I remembered the first time I heard someone refer to me as an orphan. It happened on the playground at school. I was in the fourth grade and we were outside at recess. There was a small sidewalk the girls used for hopscotch and we often partnered up. When one of the girls, Blair Cummings, was left with me, she complained.

"I don't want to be with her. She's too small, and besides, she's an orphan," she remarked, and the others looked at me as if I had a wart on my nose. I remember my face became hot and tears felt like boiling drops under my eyelids. I turned and ran away. Later, when our teacher, Miss Walker, found me sitting alone in a corner of the playground, she asked if I was sick.

"Yes," I said. It was a convenient way to escape any more ridicule. "I have a stomachache."

She sent me to the nurse's office and I was told to lie quietly after the nurse had taken my temperature even though she found that I didn't have a fever. I suppose that was why people thought of me as sickly. Whenever I felt singled out, I would often get these "stomachaches" and be thankful for the excuse to disappear. Being an orphan made me want to be invisible.

"Most of Madame Malisorf's pupils," Celine continued, "come from the finest families, people of culture who have raised their children in a world of music and art and dance. They have a head start, but don't you worry, dear," she added, reaching out to touch my cheek. "You have me and that, that is a much better head start than any of the more fortunate ones have had."

After dinner I sat with her and Sanford and listened to Celine's descriptions of some of the dances in which she had performed.

"Madame Malisorf compared me to Anna Pavlova. Have you ever heard of her?" Celine asked. I hadn't of course. She shook her head and sighed. "It's a crime, a crime that someone like you, someone who is a diamond in the rough, has been denied so much, denied the opportunity. Thank Heaven I saw you that day," she declared.

No one had ever even suggested I had any sort of talent, much less thought of me as a diamond in the rough. When I left Celine that night and went to my room, I stood in front of my full-length mirror in my new pointe shoes and my leotards and studied my tiny body, hoping to see something that would convince me I was special. All I saw was an underdeveloped little girl with big, frightened eyes.

I crawled into bed that night terrified over what was to come.

The next morning after breakfast, Sanford took me to the Peabody School, a private school. The principal was a woman named Mrs. Williams. She was tall but not too thin, with light brown hair neatly styled. I thought she had a very warm, friendly smile, and was nothing like the principal in my former school, Mr. Saks, who seemed always to be grouchy and unhappy, and who was always anxious to punish students for violating one rule or another. Often he perched in the corridors like a hawk watching and waiting. He was always charging in and out of the bathrooms, hoping to catch someone smoking.

Peabody was a much smaller school, and also much cleaner and newer. I was surprised when I was brought to a classroom where there were only eight other students, three boys and five girls. For my grade there was one teacher, Miss London, who taught English and history, and another teacher, Mr. Wiles, who taught math and science. Our physical education teacher, Mrs. Grant, also taught health education. I discovered there were only 257 students in the whole school.

"The classes are so small you know you're going to get special attention here," Sanford told me. He was right. All of my teachers were very nice and took the time to explain what I had to do in order to catch up with my classmates.

What I liked most of all was that I was enrolled and introduced to the other students as Janet Delorice, and no one was told that I had been adopted and had been an orphan before this. Everyone simply assumed I was transferring from another private school, and I did nothing to cause them to think otherwise.

I thought most of the girls were snobby as well as most of the boys, but one boy, Josh Brown, who wasn't all that much taller or bigger than me, gave me the warmest smile and greeting when I sat next to him in my first class. Afterward, he walked with me and told me about the school and the teachers. The color of his hair was so similar to mine, we could have been brother and sister. He didn't look like me, however. He had dark brown eyes and a round face with firmer lips and a nose that tipped up at the end. When he smiled, I thought he was cute, although I didn't dare say so.

"Did your parents just move here?" he asked me between classes.

"No. My father owns a glass factory," I told

him as I thought of ways to avoid telling him I had come from an orphanage.

He thought a moment and nodded.

"Yeah, I know where it is." He seemed satisfied with my answer and I was happy to let the conversation drop.

Later in the day, the girls asked more questions, and I could see that one girl, Jackie Clark, was suspicious.

"You didn't attend a private school before, did you?" she pursued.

"No," I admitted hesitantly. I was really going to have to get better at creating a story for myself.

"Were you a problem child?" Betty Lowe asked quickly.

"No," I said.

"You didn't get into big trouble?" Jackie followed.

I shook my head.

"How are your grades, pretty bad?" Betty asked with a nod and a smile as if she hoped they were.

"No. I have good grades," I told her.

They looked at each other, confused and skeptical.

"Why weren't you in a private school before, then?" Jackie demanded.

I shrugged.

"My parents just decided," I said vaguely.

"I'd rather be in a public school," Betty admitted.

"Not me," Jackie responded, and they got into their own argument and forgot about me for the moment. That was when Josh offered to show me around some more and we left the others. I enjoyed my first day at my new school so much, maybe because of Josh, that I nearly forgot Madame Malisorf would be waiting for me when I got home.

At the end of the school day Sanford was waiting in front of the school to bring me home.

"There may be times when I'll have to have one of my employees pick you up, Janet. Whoever it is will be very nice," he assured me. "Oh, and you don't have to tell Celine, she never understands why sometimes work needs to come first. I enjoy taking a break to come get you, but I just won't be able to do it every day. Don't worry, Celine won't find out, it'll be our little secret."

I tried not to worry about there being yet another secret between us, another secret kept from Celine, and concentrated on the drive. There was some roadwork being done between our home and the school, and we got stuck in a traffic jam about a mile from the school. I didn't think it was so terrible, but Sanford was getting very nervous. He kept muttering, "Damn, damn," under his breath, and chastising himself for not taking a detour. Finally, we were sailing along again. He drove a lot faster and I couldn't help thinking about the terrible car accident he and Celine had been in. The wheels squealed as we turned up the drive and came to an abrupt stop in front of the house.

I carried my new books in my arms and hurried

to the front door with him. Celine was waiting in the entryway, sitting in her wheelchair and scowling at us as if she had been waiting at the door for hours.

"Why are you so late?" she demanded as soon as we entered the house.

"Roadwork," Sanford began to explain. "It—"

"I don't have time for your excuses, Sanford. Just go on back to your precious factory." She spat the words through clenched teeth and then turned her angry face to me. "Janet, Madame Malisorf is waiting in the studio. Put your books down—come along."

I placed my books on the entryway table, gazed at Sanford with wide, frightened eyes, and then started after Celine. My heart was pounding as I entered the studio. The first thing that astounded me was how small Madame Malisorf was. From the way Celine had described her, I pictured a towering figure at least as impressive as Mrs. McGuire. Madame Malisorf looked to be no more than five feet tall. Her hair was all gray and her face was full of wrinkles, but she had such a trim, athletic body, she looked like a young person who had prematurely aged. Her eyes washed over me as I followed Celine across the floor.

Madame Malisorf wore her hair pinned up in a huge twist. She wore black leotards and pointe shoes like the ones Celine had bought for me. Her lips were scarlet and her eyes were charcoal smudges in her pale, pale face.

"Janet, this is Madame Malisorf," Celine said,

and I was amazed to hear that she no longer sounded angry. It was as if crossing the threshold of the studio transformed her.

"Hello," I said and smiled weakly.

She simply stared at me and then turned to Celine.

"You know I don't like to put girls onto full pointe until they are thirteen, Celine, no matter how long they've studied."

"She'll be thirteen very shortly, Madame," Celine said.

Madame Malisorf smirked with skepticism.

"She looks no more than nine or ten."

"I know. She's small but she's precious and very talented," Celine said.

"We'll see. I want you to walk to the far wall and back," Madame Malisorf commanded.

I gazed at Celine, who smiled and nodded encouragement. Then I walked to the wall, turned, and walked back.

"Well, Madame?" Celine asked quickly. It was obvious she expected Madame Malisorf to agree with her assessment of me.

"She does have good posture and balance. The neck looks a bit weak, but that will be rectified quickly. Stand on your toes," she ordered, and I did. When I started to lower myself, she barked, "No, stay there until I tell you otherwise."

I did what she asked and waited. My calves began to shake and to ache, but I held myself up. I could feel my face turning red.

"Hold your arms straight out," she ordered.

I did that, too.

"Keep your head high, your eyes straight ahead."

It felt like some sort of torture, but because Celine was watching me with that smile on her face, I forced myself to endure. My whole body began to shake. I hoped it would be easier in pointe shoes.

"Relax," Madame Malisorf said. "Good strength, good balance for someone without any training. You might be right, Celine," she said, "but it will take a grand effort. As far as pointe work, we'll see how long it will take to get her ready." She turned back to me. "Change into your exercise outfit and be back in ten minutes," she ordered.

There was that ten minutes again. Celine nodded at me and I hurried out and up the stairs to my room to get into my leotards. Celine was right about how Madame Malisorf conducted her class. She demonstrated and then put me into one exercise after another at the barre. Repetition was the magic word. She barked her orders and expected me to obey instantly. If I paused to catch my breath, she sighed deeply and said, "Well?" And Celine would give a little cough from the doorway where she was sitting. She hadn't told me she was going to watch my lessons and was making me even more nervous. I performed each move so many times, I thought I would do each of the exercises in my sleep. Finally, Madame Malisorf had me move away from the barre and work on standing with my feet turned out.

"For various reasons having to do with the structure of the hip joint," she explained, "a dancer can obtain the greatest extension if the leg is rotated outward, away from its usual position. This rotation will enable you to move to the side as readily as to the front or back. This position is known as—"

"Turnout," I said quickly. I wanted to impress her with my knowledge.

"Yes," she said, but she didn't seem surprised or even very pleased. Instead, she looked annoyed that I had finished her sentence. From her reflection in the mirror I could see Celine's eyes fill with warning and I moved quickly into the position as it had been described in the book.

"No, no," Madame Malisorf cried. "You don't begin from the ankles. You do not force your feet into that position and let everything from there on up follow. Turnout begins at the hip joint."

She seized me at the waist and had me do it repeatedly until I satisfied her. It was too soon in my training to go on to jumps so we returned to the barre for more exercise.

"I will get you strong enough so you can attempt the moves I will teach you," she said confidently.

When we finished for the day, I was aching all over, especially in my hips and legs. The pain was so deep in places, it made my eyes tear, but I dared not utter a syllable of complaint. All the while as I worked with Madame Malisorf, Celine watched from her wheelchair, nodding and smiling after everything Madame Malisorf said.

"She'll be wonderful, absolutely wonderful, won't she, Madame Malisorf?" Celine asked at the end of the session.

"We shall see," Madame Malisorf replied, her eyes cold and critical.

"I have already fitted her for pointe shoes."

"We can't rush her along, Celine," Madame Malisorf snapped. "You, of all people, should know that."

"We won't, but she'll progress rapidly," Celine said undaunted. "I'll see to it. She'll practice and practice, Madame."

"I should hope so," she said directly to me. "You can't expect to become a dancer with only our sessions." She thought a moment and added, "Next time, I think I'll bring another pupil along." She turned to Celine. "It's good to have someone else work alongside her."

"Yes, yes, fine," Celine said. "Thank you. Tomorrow then?"

"Tomorrow," Madame Malisorf replied, and began to gather her things.

Tomorrow? Will I have lessons every day? I wondered. When will my poor little body have a chance to recuperate?

As soon as Madame Malisorf left, Celine wheeled over to me, her eyes blazing with excitement.

"She likes you. I know she does. I've known her a long time. If she didn't think you had potential, she would simply refuse to be your dance instructor. She doesn't waste her time on mediocre students, and for her to volunteer to bring along another one of her special students . . . well, you just don't understand what that means, Janet. That must be why you're not as excited as you should be. You have to be excited, Janet. Don't you see? Madame agrees with me. You're going to be a prima ballerina. This is wonderful, wonderful," she said, clapping her hands.

I tried to smile through my aches and pains. It made her laugh.

"Don't worry about your pains, Janet. Go soak in a hot tub before dinner. After a few more sessions, you won't be so sore. You'll see. Oh, I can't wait to tell Sanford about the lesson. I was right. I knew it. I was right," she said, spinning around in her chair and wheeling toward the doorway.

What had I done to make her so confident, I wondered, besides parading across the studio, rising up on my toes, balancing myself, and then performing some vigorous exercises that left me feeling like I'd been hit by a truck?

I followed her out and walked up the stairway to my room much slower than I had the day before. It wasn't until I was in my room and the door was closed that I permitted myself my first groan. Then I ran water for a bath and soaked my sore muscles. Later, at dinner, my work in the studio with Madame Malisorf was all Celine would discuss. Sanford tried to ask me questions about my first day at school, but Celine continually interrupted with advice about this and that work at the barre.

"I wish you could have been there to see her,

Sanford. At times I felt like I was looking at myself in the mirror when my mother used to come around to watch me, too," she added.

I wondered when I was to meet my new grandparents, but there was no mention of their visit or our visiting them.

Celine wanted me to remain with her after dinner and talk about dance some more, but Sanford reminded her that I had to catch up on a great deal of schoolwork.

"Schoolwork," she said disdainfully. "Someday and someday soon, she'll have a tutor, just as I had."

"You mean you stopped going to school?" I asked.

"Of course. Dance was everything to me, and it will be to you, Janet. You'll see," she predicted.

Just dance and have a tutor all the time, I wondered, but what about friends and parties and most of all, boyfriends? I didn't look very enthusiastic about it, I guess. Her mouth turned down in a frown.

"What's wrong?" she asked quickly.

"She's very tired, Celine," Sanford answered for me. "This has been a big day, one of the biggest in her life, I imagine."

Celine studied me a moment and then smiled.

"Yes, yes, I'm sure that's it. Go do your schoolwork, dear, and then get some beauty sleep."

I was excused and returned to my room. For a moment I just sat at my desk and gazed at the small mountain of reading I had to do. Getting a new home and a new family wasn't as easy as I'd always dreamed it would be.

When I stretched against the back of my chair, my lower back and the backs of my legs screamed out in pain. I looked at myself in the mirror and groaned. I had some news for my tired little body.

"There'll be much more pain to come."

Six

Madame Malisorf kept her promise. The next day when Sanford brought me home from school, there was an older boy waiting in the studio with her. I don't know why, but I expected the student she was bringing along for my lessons to be another girl. The sight of a boy in his tights took me by such surprise, I simply stood there gaping stupidly at him. He had to be at least fifteen or sixteen, and was at least six inches taller than me with raven black hair and eyes that glittered like black onyx. He had a dark complexion, but his mouth was so red, it looked like he was wearing lipstick. It didn't look like there was an ounce of fat on his body.

He had muscular shoulders and very muscular legs. His tights fit him like a second skin, so that there wasn't much left to my imagination. Sex talk was often the topic of conversation for the older girls at the orphanage, and I couldn't help but want to listen in on their experiences. Through what they'd told me and what I overheard, I thought I knew everything I was supposed to know at my age, despite not having an older sister or mother to take me aside to discuss the birds and the bees. However, I had never been in the same room with an older boy who looked so . . . so naked. I couldn't help blushing. I saw immediately that my embarrassment annoyed him, so I shifted my eyes away.

"This is Dimitri Rocmalowitz," Madame Malisorf said. "He is one of my best students and often instructs new students on the basics. Of course, he has a way to go, but he is a very talented and precise dancer. When he tells you to do something, you should treat him with the same respect and regard you would treat me. Do you understand, Janet?"

"Yes, Madame," I replied skeptically. Dimitri looked too young to be such an amazing dancer. It would be strange taking direction from him.

"Watching someone who has mastered as much as Dimitri has will help you understand what is expected of you," she continued. "Today and from now on, I want you to begin our sessions wearing these leg warmers," she added as she handed me a bright purple pair of heavy wool leg warmers.

After I put them on we proceeded immediately to the barre and I noticed that Celine had wheeled herself into the corner of the room, where she sat with her hands folded on her lap and watched.

Dimitri went right into a warmup drill and for a moment all I could do was watch. He didn't seem shy or nervous to be dancing in front of us. It was as if he was in his own world. His legs moved with such grace and speed while he held his body in a perfectly vertical line.

"Begin," Madame Malisorf said, and I approached the barre, standing just a few feet from Dimitri. "No, don't hold the barre that tightly," she said. "See how Dimitri uses it only for balance."

I tried to relax and we began a series of exercises that included the *pliés,* the *tendus,* and the *glissés,* all that she had shown me the day before. From there we moved to the *fondus* and then the *ronds de jambe à terre.* First, Madame Malisorf would describe what she wanted. Then Dimitri would demonstrate, always with a proud look on his face as if he was dancing for an audience of thousands, and then I would begin, usually followed by Madame Malisorf's quick, "No, no, no. Dimitri, again. Watch him, Janet. Study the way he is holding his back and his neck."

Sometimes it took me so long to satisfy her, I was practically in tears before she let me go on to something else, always with the conditional statement, "We'll work on that." There wasn't anything I wouldn't be working on, seemingly forever and ever, I thought.

When we got to the turnout again, the pain of rotating my hips nearly made me cry out in pain. I was sure my face revealed all my new aches. Madame Malisorf seemed merciless, however.

Just when I thought there would be a short break so I could catch my breath, she was on to something new with Dimitri demonstrating and then me trying to mimic his moves.

The session lasted longer than the one we had the day before. I was sweating so much, I felt the dampness in my leotards, which were now glued to my skin. Finally, Madame Malisorf did give us a short break and I collapsed to the floor. Madame Malisorf went to talk to Celine and Dimitri finally looked at me for the first time since we'd been in the room.

"Why do you want to be a ballet dancer?" he asked immediately and with a sharpness in his tone that made me feel guilty.

"My mother thinks I should be," I said defensively.

"That's your reason?" he asked with a smirk. He wiped his face with his towel and then threw the soggy towel at me. "You're dripping," he said gruffly.

I found a dry spot on the towel and wiped my face and the back of my neck.

"I think I'll like it," I said cautiously. Again, he smirked.

"Ballet requires complete and utter devotion, a total commitment of mind, body, and soul. It becomes your religion. An instructor like Madame Malisorf is your high priestess, your god, her words gospel. You have to think and walk like a dancer, eat and breathe it. There is nothing else that is half as important. Then, and maybe then, you have a chance to become a real dancer."

"I don't expect to become a famous dancer," I said and wondered why this boy made me feel like I had to defend myself . . . especially when I wasn't so sure that I even wanted to be a dancer.

He looked quickly toward Madame Malisorf and Celine and then back at me.

"Don't ever let Madame Malisorf hear you say such a weak, self-defeating thing. She'll turn and walk out of the room forever," he warned.

My heart, which was pounding madly from our exercises anyway, stopped and then pounded even harder. Celine would be devastated. She would hate me, I thought.

"Madame Malisorf will tell you what you will and will not be," he continued and then he shook his head. "Another spoiled rich child whose parents think she's someone special," he commented disdainfully.

"I am not," I said, nearly in tears.

"No? How many kids your age have a studio like this in their homes and a teacher who costs thousands of dollars a week?"

"Thousands?" I gulped.

"Of course, you little idiot. Don't you know who she is?" He groaned. "This isn't going to last long. I can just feel it," he said with a knowing shake of his head.

"Yes, it will. I'll do what I have to do and I'll do it well," I fired back at him.

I didn't want to tell him that I thought my life depended on it; that the woman who wanted to love me as a mother had her heart set on my success as a dancer and that I would devote all my strength and energy toward making her happy.

"My mother was going to be a famous dancer until she was in a terrible car accident. That's why we have this studio. It's not here just for me."

He smirked.

"You shouldn't look down on someone who is just starting out simply because you're a good ballet student," I added.

He finally smiled.

"How could I do anything but look down at you? What are you, four feet eight?"

This time tears escaped the corners of my eyes. I turned my back on him and wiped them away quickly.

"Are you really nearly thirteen?" he continued. His voice had softened and I wondered if he was sorry he'd hurt my feelings.

I began to answer him when Madame Malisorf returned and told me to take off the leg warmers. It was time to move away from the barre to repeat everything we had done, but this time without the aid of the barre. I couldn't help being tired and making mistakes. I knew I was looking very clumsy and awkward. Every time Madame Malisorf corrected me, Dimitri shook his head and smirked. Then, as if to drive home his disdain, he would do what she asked so perfectly, showing off, his spinning turns so fast he became a blur. Occasionally he would break out of the spin and do a leap that seemed to defy gravity and land without a sound. Whenever he demonstrated something for me, Madame Malisorf would cry, "That's it! That's what I want. Study him. Watch him. Someday you must be as good as he is."

His face filled with arrogant pride as he puffed out his chest toward me.

I wanted to say I'd rather watch a dead fish floating on the top of our lake, but held my breath and my words and tried again. Finally, mercifully, it seemed, the session ended. Celine clapped and wheeled herself to the center of the studio.

"Bravo, bravo. What a beautiful beginning. Thank you, Madame Malisorf. Thank you. And Dimitri, you make me want to get up out of this chair, forget my crippled legs, and dance in your arms."

He bowed.

"Madame Malisorf has told me how wonderfully you danced and what a tragedy it was for ballet when you were injured, Mrs. Delorice."

"Yes," Celine said softly, her eyes taking on that faraway, distant look. Then she smiled toward me. "But my daughter will do what I can't do anymore. Don't you agree?"

He looked at me.

"Perhaps," he said with that crooked smile on his lips. "If she learns to be dedicated, devoted, and obedient."

"She will," Celine promised and I wondered if just her command would turn me into a ballerina as easily as it had turned a cloudy, gloomy day bright and beautiful.

I tried not to look as tired and as sore as I was,

but Dimitri saw through my mask and smiled cruelly at me. When I entered my room, I threw myself on my bed and let my tears burst forth freely.

I'll never be the dancer Celine dreams I'll become, I thought. I may never be the daughter she wants, but I'd rather die trying than disappoint her.

Once again at dinner all our conversation centered around the dance class and my progress. Celine talked so much she barely ate or took breaths between sentences. Sanford tried to talk about other things, but she refused to change the subject. He smiled at her and at me, his face filled with amusement. Afterward, he pulled me aside to tell me that it had been some time since Celine was as animated and cheerful.

"Thank you for making Celine so happy, Janet. You're a wonderful addition to our family. Thank you for just being who you are," he said. He smiled a genuine smile and I couldn't help but think that this smile looked so much better than the tight, grim one he usually wore around Celine.

Celine caught up to us in the hallway and noticed Sanford's beaming smile. "Why are you grinning like an idiot, Sanford? What are you two discussing?" Suddenly her eyes narrowed and turned dark and cold. "Janet, go to your room. You need your rest. You're obviously going to need all the help you can get to keep up with Dimitri."

I couldn't help but feel that Celine had scolded me and I moped up to my room to collapse.

The first two weeks of my new life flew by so quickly, they felt like hours. I was sure it was because each and every moment of my day was full of things to do. Unlike in the orphanage, there weren't long hours of emptiness to fill with distractions and daydreams. Here I was working on my school assignments, taking dance lessons, recuperating from them, and starting over again. I went to sleep early and ate from the strict dancer's diet Celine had designed. Although I thought it was too early to see any real changes, I believed my legs were stronger, my small muscles tighter. I even thought I was doing what Dimitri claimed I would have to do: walk and move like a dancer, even when I wasn't in the studio.

Because my after-school time was dedicated to dance lessons, it was hard to make new friends and Celine wouldn't permit me to join any teams or clubs.

"All we need is for you to sustain some sort of injury now," she said. She even tried to get me out of gym class, but the school wouldn't permit it and Sanford argued that it wouldn't interfere with my dancing lessons.

"Of course it will," Celine snapped. "I don't want her wasting her physical energies on nonsense."

"It isn't nonsense, darling," he tried to explain, but Celine would have none of it. She hadn't gotten her way and she didn't like it one bit.

"Don't do any more than you have to," she advised me, "and do what I used to do whenever you can: claim you have cramps from your period."

"But I haven't gotten my period yet," I reminded her.

"So what? Who's going to know? Lying," she said when she saw the expression on my face, "is all right if it's for the right cause. I'll never punish you for doing something to protect your dancing, Janet, never, no matter what," she said, her eyes so bright and big, they scared me. I wondered where she went when that look came over her.

Like most of the girls and boys my age at the orphanage, I used to fantasize about the people who would become my parents. I filled my head with dreams of fun things like picnics and trips to the park, and I saw myself holding my father's hand as we walked through the gates of Disneyland. I imagined big, beautiful birthday parties, and I even dreamed of having little brothers and sisters.

How empty and different the big house I now lived in seemed when I compared it to the house in my dreams. Yes, I had expensive things and a room bigger than I'd ever seen, and there was a lake and beautiful grounds, but none of the family closeness or trips or fun and games that I'd imagined. Sanford wanted to spend time with me, to show off his factory, but Celine just seemed to come up with one reason after another why I couldn't go. Finally, she realized how silly her arguments sounded and relented. I went to work with Sanford on a Saturday and saw the machines and the products. I met some of his workers and his executives. I was amazed at how pleasant and eager he was to show me things and how sad I was when our time alone ended. I think Sanford felt the same way—on the ride home neither of us spoke and for the first time that day the mood between us was gloomy.

When we returned home and I started to tell Celine about our day, she grimaced as if in pain.

"We need the factory so that we can afford the luxuries in life," she said. "What we *don't* need is to acknowledge its existence. And we certainly don't allow it to take up one iota of our time or thought."

"But some of the things that are made in the factory are beautiful, aren't they?" I asked.

"I suppose, in a pedestrian sort of way," she admitted, although I didn't understand exactly what she meant, and I saw it displeased Sanford. She didn't become animated and happy again until Sanford told her he had gotten us tickets to the Metropolitan Ballet's performance of *The Four Temperaments*.

"Now," she cried, "now you will see your first real ballet and understand what it is I want you to do and become."

Celine had Sanford take us to buy me a formal dress. I chose a long royal blue taffeta and Celine even had Sanford buy me some jewelry—a set of sapphire earrings and a matching teardrop-shaped necklace.

"Going to the ballet is a very special thing," she

explained. "Everyone wears their very best clothes. You'll see."

She brought me to a salon where they styled my hair in a French twist and showed me how to apply makeup properly. When I gazed at myself in the mirror, I was amazed at how grown-up I looked.

"I want you to make a statement, to be noticed, to be someone everyone will look at and think, 'there's an up-and-coming star, a little princess.'"

I had to admit I was finally swept away in Celine's world. I permitted myself to dream the same dreams, to think of myself as a celebrity, my name up in lights, and when I saw the theater and all those rich and elegant-looking people in the audience, I was filled with excitement, too. By the time the curtain lifted, my heart was pounding. The ballet began. I gazed at my new mother beside me in her wheelchair, saw the happiness and radiance in her eyes, and felt as if I was leaping and soaring alongside her. During the first act, she reached through the darkness until she found my hand.

When I turned to her she whispered, "Someday, Janet, Sanford and I will be coming here to see you."

"Someday," she whispered, lost in her dream.

And I dared to believe it could come true.

Seven

Although I didn't hear them referred to very much, I couldn't help wondering when I would meet my grandparents, Celine's mother and father. I never heard or saw her talking to them on the phone and neither she nor Sanford mentioned speaking to them recently or on any regular basis. During the week, Sanford and I usually ate breakfast without Celine since it took her much longer to rise and dress. I knew Sanford would tell me about my new grandparents if I asked him, but I was having trouble getting up the nerve. Finally I decided I would settle into my routine and wait for Celine to bring up the subject of her parents again—then I would ask to meet them.

As the days wore on, my dance lessons seemed to be going better, and although I couldn't imagine myself ever liking Dimitri, I couldn't help being flattered when he complimented me on my technique. Madame Malisorf didn't go so far as to say I was a special student, but she did offer that I was better than average, which was enough to make Celine happy and even more confident.

"I think," Celine said one night at dinner, "that it's time for my mother to see Janet. Janet's made significant progress. I'll have mother stop by during one of her dance lessons."

Sanford nodded without speaking, but I saw something strange in his eyes, a look of concern that I hadn't seen often before. Of course, I couldn't help wondering why I hadn't met Celine's parents before now. I knew they didn't live very far away. Why didn't we ever visit? I kicked myself for not having the courage to ask Sanford earlier since it was obvious from the look on his face that he had strong opinions about them.

"Isn't your brother returning from his holiday tomorrow?" Sanford asked her. His face didn't relax at all, and I wondered what it was about Celine's family that upset him.

"I don't recall. And what do you mean, return from his holiday? When isn't Daniel on holiday?" she asked and laughed a high, thin laugh.

Nothing else was said about Celine's family, but two days afterward, right in the middle of our dinner, the doorbell sounded and Mildred hurried out of the kitchen to see who it was. Minutes later, I heard a loud laugh.

"Mildred, you're still here! Wonderful!" A loud voice boomed from the entryway.

"Daniel," Celine moaned, shaking her head.

Moments later, Celine's younger brother burst

into the dining room. His light brown hair was long and tossed about his head and face as if he had been running his fingers through it for hours. Not quite six feet tall with an athletic build, Daniel had hazel eyes set in a face much more chiseled than Celine's. I saw resemblances in their noses and mouths, but there was a sly smile on his lips that I would discover to be a habitual characteristic. He wore a black leather jacket, faded blue jeans, and black boots, as well as black leather gloves.

"Celine, Sanford," he cried. "How are you?" He started to take off his gloves. "I'm in time for dinner. What luck. I'm starving."

He slid into the chair across from me and reached for some bread before anyone could respond.

"Hello, Daniel," Celine said dryly. "Please meet Janet."

He winked at me.

"I heard you guys were finally parents. Mother gave me an earful." He studied me. "How are they treating you? Has Sanford negotiated your allowance yet? Better let me represent you. Ah, a veal roast," he said, stabbing a piece of meat. "Mildred's quite a good cook." He shoved the meat into his mouth and chewed.

It was as if a strong, wild wind had blown into the house. Sanford was so obviously stunned by Daniel's appearance that he sat with his hand frozen in the air, his fork full of peas.

"Hello, Daniel," Sanford said, his eyes softening. "I see you finally got that motorcycle you've been threatening to buy."

"You bet I did," Daniel said. "I seem to remember you used to throw around the idea of getting one of your own."

"I was never really serious," he said, glancing at Celine.

"How about you?" Daniel asked me. "You want to go for a ride after dinner?"

"Of course she doesn't," Celine said quickly. "Do you think I would place her in such danger?"

Daniel laughed and continued to eat. I was still too surprised and overwhelmed to speak. He winked at me again.

"I bet you'd like a ride," he said, and he stared at me so intently it seemed like he could see into my soul. I wondered if my soul wore biker leather!

"Stop it, Daniel," Celine ordered. He laughed again and shook his head in defeat.

"Where were you this time?" Sanford asked. Although he meant it to sound critical, I saw a look of envy in his eyes as he waited for Daniel to tell about his adventures.

"The Cape. You would have loved it, Sanford. We took the sea route through Connecticut and rode along the ocean. I swear, with the wind blowing through our hair and the smell of the fresh salt air, I felt like we could drive forever. Never come back."

"And yet here you are. I dare not ask who the *we* was," Celine said as she wrinkled up her nose.

"You dare not? Funny, Mother dared not either."

"I'll bet," Sanford said with a small smile.

"Actually, Sanford, she was a very pretty young damsel in distress when I found her, clothed and fed her, and bought her a motorcycle," Daniel told him between bites.

"You bought a strange woman a motorcycle?" Celine asked with a grimace.

"Actually, she wasn't so strange after a few days," Daniel said and winked at me again. "So, tell me all about yourself, Janet. How old are you?"

"I'll be thirteen in a few weeks," I said hesitantly. Daniel seemed larger than life and having him concentrate his questions on me was making me nervous.

"That old? You'll need to negotiate a retirement package as well then," he joked. "Seriously, are they treating you well here? Because if they're not, I have friends in high places and I can have things going your way in no time. They have to obey the rules of the Geneva Convention when it comes to prisoners."

"But . . . but I'm not a prisoner," I said quickly, looking from Sanford to Celine for help.

"Will you stop it. You'll frighten her with your behavior," Celine said. She paused and then asked, "How are Mother and Father?"

"Proper well," he said. He turned to me. "Our parents are slowly becoming statues. They sit still as granite and breathe only filtered air."

"Daniel!" Celine chastised.

"They're fine, they're fine. Of course, I saw them only for a few minutes before Mother started in on you know what," he said, nodding toward me.

"That's enough," Sanford said sharply.

"She should know what she's in for, what sort of family she has contracted to do business with, don't you think?" Daniel replied.

"Please," Celine pleaded. He shrugged.

"Okay, I'll be civil. Really. How do you like life here, Janet?" he asked me.

"I like it a lot," I said.

"And they put you in that snobby school?"

"Peabody is not a snobby school. It's a special school with advantages," Celine corrected.

"Did they tell you I went there but I was asked to please seek another place for my studies?"

I shook my head.

"My brother," Celine explained, "is what is generally known as a spoiled brat. No matter how much money my parents were willing to spend on him or what they were willing to do, he always managed to spoil it," she said, glaring at him.

"I always did choke on that silver spoon," he said with another shrug. "Mildred," he called when she appeared, "you've outdone yourself with this veal. It's as succulent as a virgin's lips," he said, smacking his own lips together. Mildred turned bright pink.

"Daniel!" Celine cried.

"Just trying to be complimentary," he said, "and appreciative." He leaned toward me to whisper loudly. "My sister always complains that I'm not appreciative."

I looked at Sanford, who put his silverware down a little harder than usual.

"How are things at the printing company, Daniel?" Sanford asked.

Daniel straightened in his chair and wiped his mouth with a napkin.

"Well, when I left for my vacation, we were down five percent from this period last year, which raised father's blood pressure five percent, but when I stopped by late today to pick up my mail, he told me we had been given the Glenn golf clubs account and that spiked us back to where we were, so his blood pressure improved. I swear his heart is connected to the Dow-Jones. If there's a crash, it's curtains," he said, slicing his forefinger across his Adam's apple.

"You can ridicule him all you want, Daniel, but he built a successful business for you and a comfortable life for both of us," Celine scolded.

"Yes, yes, I suppose so. I'm just having fun," he confessed to me. "Something my brother-in-law here doesn't have much of because he works too hard. All work and no play, Sanford," he warned. Then he gazed at me. "So," he said, "you're taking dance lessons, I hear."

"Yes," I said softly.

"And she's doing very well," Celine added.

"That's nice." He sat back. "I must say, sister dear, you and Mr. Glass chose a little gem here. I'm impressed, Sanford."

"We're very fond of Janet and we hope she's growing fond of us," Sanford replied, and I was glad to see him smile.

"Are you?" Daniel asked me with that impish twinkle in his eyes.

"Yes," I said quickly.

He laughed.

"Are you sure I can't take her for a little ride on the cycle?"

"Absolutely sure," Celine said. "If you want to go out and be reckless, I can't stop you, but you won't be reckless with my daughter," she told him. "Not now," she added, "now that she's on the threshold of becoming someone very special."

"Really?" Daniel said, gazing at me across the table. He smiled. "I would have thought she was already someone special. Even before she came here," he added, dazzling me with his smile.

I couldn't help liking him even though Celine's expression and harsh words made it clear she disapproved.

After dinner Daniel and Sanford went off to the den to talk and Celine and I went to the living room, where she apologized for her brother's behavior.

"Your new uncle is really good-hearted, but he's just a bit lost at the moment. We're doing our best to help him," she said. "It's difficult. His problem is he hasn't any goals. He has no focus, and that's the most important thing to have in life, Janet, focus and determination. He doesn't want anything enough to sacrifice and suffer some pain. He's too selfish and indulgent," she continued.

She gazed up at her own portrait above the mantel and sighed.

"We came from the same home, had the same

parents, but sometimes, sometimes, he seems like a stranger to me."

"Did he ever want to dance, too?" I asked.

"Daniel?" she laughed. "Daniel has two left feet and he doesn't have the attention span to learn a single exercise. But," she said sighing again, "he's my brother. I have to love him."

Then she looked at me.

"And you're my hope," she said. "I will always love you."

Knowing that Celine's eyes were always following me and that I was her hope made me try harder, but it also made me feel worse if I didn't please Madame Malisorf or make progress as fast as I was expected to make it. The day after my uncle Daniel's explosive introduction, Celine had a doctor's appointment that ran late and kept her from attending my dance lesson after school. Without her sitting there in the corner, I felt a little more at ease, and even Dimitri seemed friendlier. Toward the end of the lesson, Madame Malisorf declared that tomorrow she would start me on pointe.

"I don't understand why she's doing that," Dimitri declared after she had left for her next lesson. He was old enough to drive and had his own car. "She's the most demanding dance instructor in the area and doesn't easily put a student on pointe. Certainly never this early." He thought a moment. "She's probably just satisfying your mother. Your feet aren't even properly developed."

"They are too," I said looking down at them to see if he was right.

He wiped his face with the towel and stared at me. "I've always liked to watch young girls develop," he said suddenly.

The way he was gazing at me made me very self-conscious. My leotards were as tight as his, and for the first time I was embarrassed by how much they revealed.

"Are you developing breasts or is that just some baby fat?" he asked, jabbing his finger toward me.

My breath caught in my throat and I jumped away from his reach.

"You know, I've heard there's an avant-garde group of dancers who dance naked. Wanna try it?" he asked. After what he'd just done, I had no idea if he was kidding me or not.

"Naked?" I couldn't imagine such a thing.

"It's supposed to give you more freedom of expression. I really might try it one of these days," he said. "Well?"

"Well what?"

"You didn't answer my question, breasts or baby fat?"

"That's very personal," I mumbled.

"You shouldn't be ashamed of your body," he continued.

"I'm not ashamed."

"Do I look like I'm ashamed of mine? Am I hiding anything from you? That's right, look at me," he said, turning so he faced me fully. He smiled. "I remember how you looked at me that first day."

I started to shake my head.

"Don't deny it. Honesty is the most important characteristic for a dancer. Your honesty will be evident when you move. Madame Malisorf always says that. Breasts or baby fat?" he pursued. He stepped closer to me.

He smiled, his upper lip curling in to his now familiar sneer.

"I could make you look very bad here, you know. Madame will take you off pointe in seconds. I don't think your mother would appreciate that, do you?"

Tears clouded my vision.

"What do you want from me?" I cried.

"Let me decide for myself," he said and reached out to touch my chest. I was too frightened to stop him. "I'm still not sure. I'll tell you when I know," he added. I started to turn away from him, but he seized my leotard at the shoulder and began peeling it off before I could get away.

"Stop," I begged him.

"Ashamed?" He practically growled the word.

"No, but please, don't." I pleaded.

"If you don't let me see, I will ruin your first day on pointe," he threatened.

I swallowed down the lump in my throat and froze, my heart pounding as he continued to lower my leotard until he could reveal my chest. He stood there staring at me. Then, very slowly, his eyes narrow and strangely dark, he touched me. I jumped back as if his fingers were filled with electricity.

"Breasts," he concluded. "There, was that so difficult?" he asked and did a full pirouette, a leap, and a soft fall before heading out the studio door and leaving me behind, tears streaming down my cheeks, my heart pounding.

I pulled up my leotard and followed him out. I remained in the shadows of the hallway until I heard him leave the house.

"Is there anything wrong?" Mildred asked, seeing me cowering in a corner.

"No," I said. "I was just resting."

She tilted her head in confusion.

I hurried down the hall, away from her questioning eyes, up the stairs, and to my room, shutting the door behind me quickly. I was still embarrassed and frightened by the experience in the studio. My legs were actually trembling. What frightened me the most was the feeling of being trapped and helpless. He could have stripped me naked and I would have been afraid to stop him. Why did he do it? Why did he take such advantage of me? Why didn't I cry for help? At least Mildred could have come to help me.

I wiped away my tears and looked at myself in the mirror. No one had ever treated me as anything more than a little girl. No boy had ever thought of me sexually before as far as I knew. But now my breasts were budding. My time was coming. When Dimitri had touched me, I was terrified, but there was a strange new sensation as well. I wasn't sure if I was more afraid of him or what had happened inside me.

How lucky other girls were, girls who had

mothers and sisters to talk to at a moment like this, I thought. If I mentioned to Celine what had happened, it might create havoc with my dance lessons. Madame Malisorf might even walk out on us and then what would I do?

How would I keep this a secret? What would it feel like to stand across from Dimitri tomorrow? I would be nervous enough as it was auditioning to begin on pointe. I couldn't help wondering if this was the first of many more experiences I would have to endure to please Celine.

That, as much as anything else, caused me to be afraid of what tomorrow would bring.

Eight

I tossed and turned for hours that night, and when I finally did fall asleep, I had so many nightmares, I kept waking up in a cold sweat, and by morning I was actually shivering and the back of my neck ached. I fell asleep again just before I was supposed to get up and get ready for school. A soft knock at the door woke me. Sanford looked in.

"You should be getting up, Janet," he said with a smile.

I nodded and started to sit up when the ache traveled down my spine and I groaned. Sanford grew concerned and stepped into my room.

"What's wrong?"

"I don't feel so good," I complained. "My neck aches and I'm cold," I said through chattering teeth.

He put his hand on my forehead and looked even more worried.

"You feel like you have fever. I'll get a thermometer," he said and hurried out of the room. He was back in less than a minute and put the thermometer under my tongue.

"I was afraid of this," he muttered. He paced as he waited. "You've been working too hard on your schoolwork and your dancing. You need more time to rest. You're growing, too, and all this is so new and frightening for you, I'm sure. No one listens to me, but I know I'm right about this."

He looked at the thermometer and nodded.

"A hundred and one. That's a fever. You stay right there, young lady. I'm sending Mildred up with some aspirin for you. Does your throat hurt?"

I shook my head.

"No, just my neck and shoulders ache. And the backs of my legs," I added, but they were always aching so I didn't think anything special about it.

He stared at me a moment.

"I've changed my mind. I won't give you aspirins yet. I'm taking you to the doctor," he decided. "Just throw something on, anything, I'll meet you downstairs." he added and left the room.

I got up slowly, washed my face, and dressed in an old flannel shirt and a pair of loose-fitting jeans. As I passed Sanford and Celine's room, I could hear their muffled voices. Celine sounded very upset.

"What are you talking about?" I heard her say. "That's nonsense. People don't get sick from dancing too much."

"I didn't say that was the only cause. The child's exhausted."

"Nonsense. She's young. She has an unlimited well of energy," Celine insisted. I didn't have the strength to listen to more so I slowly made my way downstairs.

When Sanford joined me in the entryway, he offered to carry me to the car, but I wasn't in that much pain and I felt silly with him just holding my arm as if I were some old lady.

"I've already called Dr. Franklin. He's a good friend and he's coming into his office a little early just to see you first," Sanford explained.

"Is Celine angry at me?" I asked. She hadn't even come to see how I was.

"No, of course not. She's concerned, that's all," he said but quickly looked away.

The doctor examined me and concluded that I had the flu. He didn't prescribe anything more than aspirin and rest. Less than an hour later, I was back in my bed, taking aspirin and sipping some tea.

"I'll call from the factory," Sanford told Mildred. "Take her temperature in about two hours, okay?"

"Yes sir," she said with a smile.

I fell back to sleep and did have a better rest. I could have slept longer, but I sensed someone was in my room and opened my eyes to see Celine in her wheelchair at my bedside, staring at me.

"You don't feel very warm to me," she said, taking her hand from my forehead.

"I do feel a little better," I agreed, though I really still felt sore and tired.

"Good. Don't worry about the schoolwork. I've already called and your work will be delivered to the house later this afternoon. Rest for the remainder of the day until your dance lesson," she added.

"My dance lesson? But maybe I should wait until tomorrow, Mother," I said weakly.

"No, no, you never cancel a lesson with Madame Malisorf. She cancels you. Do you have any idea how many other people are after her to work with their sons and daughters? This is a coup, a major accomplishment getting her to concentrate on you like this, and you're doing well. She told me she had decided to put you on pointe. I'm so proud of you, dear. It took me years to go on pointe. Do you know that?"

I shook my head.

"Well, it did, so you see how talented you are."

"But I'm afraid I won't do well if I don't feel well," I moaned.

"We must never let our bodies disappoint us, Janet," she insisted. "A dancer *must* be dedicated. No matter what, when it comes time to perform, you perform. I even danced on the day my grandmother died. I was very close to her. She favored me and had a lot to do with my parents' supporting my efforts to become a ballerina. I was sad but I had to dance and that was that. If I could dance on my grandmother's day of death, you can dance with a little ache and a little fever, Janet. Right? Right?" she pursued when I didn't reply quickly enough.

"Yes," I said softly. I couldn't help but wish that Sanford was home to save me.

"Good. Then it's settled. Rest until I call for you," she said and started to wheel herself out. "Actually, this is lucky. You were able to rest all day before starting your first lesson on pointe. See? Everything works out for the dedicated," she declared and left.

She danced on the day her grandmother died, I thought. I never had a grandmother, not even a mother, but if I had them, I would love them too much not to be too sad to do anything if they died. I could never be that dedicated. Was there something wrong with me?

Mildred came to take my temperature and told me it was under a hundred. I still had a dull ache at the back of my neck and I hadn't eaten much all day. I nibbled on some toast and jelly and a few spoonfuls of hot oatmeal. My stomach churned angrily with every morsel I swallowed and I knew if I tried to eat any more it would make me sick.

Sanford sent a message that he hoped I felt better and apologized for having to remain at the factory. Mildred told me he said he had some major problems or he would have been home earlier.

I fell asleep again and then I woke to the sound of Celine's stairway elevator chair. I waited, staring at my door. Moments later she came rolling into my room.

"Time to get up, dear," she sang as if it was first thing in the morning. "Take a hot shower to warm up your muscles and put on your leotards and your pointe shoes."

I groaned as I sat up, and when I stood, I felt a bit woozy, but I tried to hide it from her. I knew that I had no choice but to dance for her.

"Just take your shower quickly," Celine ordered.

My legs felt so tight. How could I ever dance? I had trouble walking. Nevertheless, I forced myself into the shower and stood under the water, letting it stream down my neck and back. It did make me feel a little better.

"Hurry downstairs," Celine said as she left my room. "I want you to do some warm-up exercises before Madame Malisorf arrives. Dimitri is already here. He'll coach you," she added and my heart started to pound as I thought about him and his creepy eyes inspecting my body.

It nearly exhausted me to put on my leotards and shoes, but I did it. When I descended the stairs, Mildred came out of the living room where she had been dusting and polishing furniture. She looked very surprised.

"You shouldn't be out of bed, Janet." She put her arm around me and began to turn me back toward the stairs. "Mr. Delorice left me orders and—"

"My mother wants me at my dance lesson," I said.

"She does? Oh." Her tone of voice made it clear which Delorice she was more afraid of crossing.

"Janet," Celine called sharply from upstairs.

"I'm coming," I said and hurried up to the studio.

Dimitri was at the barre stretching. As usual he was totally oblivious to everyone and everything around him. I approached, took my position, and began. Finally, he looked at me.

"Today is your big day," he said. "If you're nice to me, I'll make you look good."

He laughed and broke away to do what I had already learned were *frappes* on three-quarter pointe. He made it look as easy as walking and from the smug look on his face, I knew he was showing off. His arrogant smile was beginning to make me feel sicker than the flu.

Madame Malisorf arrived within minutes and looked pleased that I had already warmed up.

"Let me see your feet," she ordered and inspected my pointe shoes. "Excellent. Well done, Celine," she told my mother, who nodded and smiled. "Pull up," she ordered.

A ballet posture that aligns the body so you stand up straight with hips level and even, shoulders open but relaxed and centered over the hips, your pelvis straight, back straight, head up, weight centered evenly between your feet, was known as *pulled up*. Madame Malisorf told me to imagine myself suspended by a thread attached to the top of my head. She said I did it well and that I had excellent posture.

"The most important thing to remember for pointe work is proper coordination of your whole body, each part adapting correctly and without strain to any new position without losing your placement, Janet," Madame Malisorf began, her nasal voice sounding haughtier than usual.

Dimitri, at her side, demonstrated. He looked like a giant puppet to me.

"We have worked hard at developing your strength. I want your knees absolutely straight like Dimitri's. I am satisfied that your ankle joint is sufficiently flexible to form with the forefoot at a right-angle when on the demi-pointe. Do not curl or clutch your toes. Dimitri," she said and again he demonstrated.

As I began the exercises and moves she ordered, she continually yelled, "Line, posture, line. No, no, no, you're sagging. Why are you acting so weak? Again, again. Dimitri," she said with frustration. "Another demonstration. Look at him, watch him, study him," she commanded. Finally she lost her patience and seized me at the shoulders and turned me toward Dimitri. "Watch him!"

He stepped right in front of me, maybe half a foot away and began.

"See how important posture is?"

"Yes, Madame," I said.

"So? Why today are you forgetting it?"

I looked at Celine. She shook her head gently. I would be permitted no excuses. I couldn't even mention my being sick. I began again, trying harder. My body shook so much inside, it felt as if my bones were rattling, but again, I kept it all hidden.

Dimitri demonstrated the ronds de jambe en

l'air, the petite and grande battements, everything with an air of superiority. The music pounded in my ears. I felt more awkward than ever, and every time I gazed at Madame Malisorf, I saw her disapproval and disappointment.

"Stop, stop, stop," she cried. "Maybe it's too soon," she muttered, shaking her head.

"No," I moaned. My ankles felt like they would snap and my toes would probably be permanently cramped, but I could not stop. My new life depended on it.

Dimitri looked at me and then stepped up beside me.

"Let's try again, Madame," he said, putting his hands on my hips. "I'll help guide her through it."

Reluctantly, she clapped her hands and we began. Dimitri whispered in my ear, explaining how I should move and which way to lean and turn. I felt different, better and safer in his strong hands. He had great strength and was practically holding me up at times.

"Better," Madame Malisorf muttered. "Yes, that's it. Good. Keep the line. Good."

I felt like a limp dishrag when the lesson finally ended. My leotards were soaked through.

"An adequate first attempt," Madame Malisorf declared, stressing the word *adequate.*

"She'll be much better tomorrow," Celine said, wheeling up to us.

"Perhaps not tomorrow but soon after," Madame Malisorf allowed.

Dimitri was sweating almost as much as me.

"Thank you for your extra effort, Dimitri," she

told him. "You should take a warm shower immediately," she added. "I don't want my prize pupil going out in the chilly air and getting sick. Celine?"

"Of course. Go up and use my shower, Dimitri. Janet, show him my room, please."

Madame Malisorf turned to Celine. "In two weeks I'm presenting a recital with my newest students and Janet will be included."

"Oh, Janet, that's wonderful. Did you hear what she said? Thank you, Madame. Thank you," Celine said. "Your first recital. How wonderful, Janet."

"Recital?" I squeaked. "You mean with an audience and everything?"

"You will be ready," Madame Malisorf declared with a small smile, "for what you will be asked to do."

"Oh yes, she'll be ready. Whatever it is, she'll be ready," Celine assured her.

Dimitri took his bag and followed me out of the studio.

"You were awful in the beginning," he said as we reached the stairway.

"I was sick. I'm still sick. I had a fever this morning," I complained.

He laughed.

"I'm glad you didn't tell Madame that. She hates excuses," he explained. "Lead the way," he added, nodding at the steps. I started up. "You know your rear end has become quite tight and round just in the short time I've been working with you."

I was too embarrassed to say anything and continued upstairs where I showed him Celine and Sanford's bathroom. After I'd given him a clean towel I hurried away to my own room to shower and crawl back into bed. My ankles ached worse than any other part of my body and when I took off my pointe shoes, my feet were covered with red blotches.

I turned on my shower and took off my leotards, but just before I stepped into the stall, I heard Dimitri say, "Pull up."

I spun around, shocked. There he was with a towel around his waist, gazing at me.

"Pull up," he said again. "Posture, posture."

"Go away!" I cried, covering myself as best I could. He laughed.

"Come on. Pull up. Remember what I told you about that group that dances naked?" He reached for my hand. I wrapped my hands around myself tightly, but he was too strong and pulled my arm away from my chest. Then, in another motion, he undid his towel and stood naked before me. I couldn't take my eyes off him, despite my shock and terror.

He went on his toes, pulled me closer, turned me around, and lifted me in the air. Then he set me down and pressed his body against me.

"There," he said. "Didn't that feel good?"

He laughed and scooped up his towel, wrapping it around his waist as he walked out of my room.

I could barely breathe.

My head was spinning. Slowly, I sank to the floor and sat there, stunned. A moment later, I thought I was going to retch. I literally crawled over to the shower and stepped into the steamy stall.

Within minutes I got out, dried myself quickly, and crawled into bed as I had planned. Just as I closed my eyes, I heard my door open and Dimitri looked in.

"Until tomorrow. Oh. And as I said, very nice and tight little rear end. You're going to be a dancer after all," he added with a laugh and was gone.

Not only couldn't I talk, I couldn't even think. I pressed my hands to my stomach and turned on my side. In moments I was asleep.

I'd only been asleep a few hours when I woke to the sound of bickering. I knew I had slept awhile because it was already dark outside. Sanford's and Celine's voices carried down the hallway. He couldn't believe she had forced me to take a lesson.

"She had a fever. Dr. Franklin said she has the flu, Celine. How could you put her through all that physical exertion?"

"You don't understand," she told him. "She has to understand obstacles, overcome them, build an inner strength. That's what makes the difference between a real dancer and an amateur, a child and a woman. She did well enough today to be invited to a recital. Didn't you hear what I said? A recital!"

"She's too young, Celine," Sanford insisted.

"No, you fool. She's almost too old. In a matter

of weeks, she's grown years. You don't know about anything but glass and that stupid factory of yours. Stick with that and leave our daughter to me. You took away my chance, but you won't take away hers," she cried.

And then there was silence.

Nine

Despite what Celine had said at dinner, I didn't get to meet my new grandparents until the day of Madame Malisorf's recital. Twice a year she held a recital to debut her new students and showcase her older ones. The new dancers like myself were given a variety of exercises and moves to demonstrate. The older ones each performed a scene from a famous ballet. Dimitri was dancing the lead in *Romeo and Juliet.*

Because I learned and practiced in my own studio, I had never met the half dozen other beginning students. Consequently they didn't know how far I had progressed and I had no idea what they could do either. When Sanford, Celine, and I arrived at Madame Malisorf's studio, the other students and I studied each other during warm-ups as if we were gunfighters soon to be in a shoot-out. From the intense expressions on the faces of the parents, grandparents, sisters and brothers, I sensed that everyone was hoping their son or daughter or sibling would look the most impressive. I knew Celine was hoping that. All the way to the studio, she bragged about me.

"When they all find out that you not only didn't have any training before you came to live with us, but you hadn't even seen a ballet, they will be amazed. And wait until they discover how quickly Madame Malisorf put you on pointe," she added with a little laugh. "I can just imagine their faces, can't you, Sanford?"

"I still think she was rushed along a bit when it came to that, Celine," he said softly. He was the only one to notice my horrible aches and pains and asked me each night if I wanted a hot pack or a massage. Sometimes it was so bad I could barely walk the next day.

"I think Madame Malisorf is the best judge of that, Sanford. If she didn't think Janet was doing well, she wouldn't want her in the recital," she insisted.

As if I wasn't nervous enough already, Celine's words and ultra-high expectations were making me tremble. Maybe because I was so nervous, my feet ached even more. They were so swollen, I could barely lace my shoes this morning.

When we got to Madame Malisorf's studio we saw that a small crowd of spectators had already arrived, made up mostly of families of the dancers, but also, according to Celine, consisting of some ballet lovers and other teachers, even ballet producers on the lookout for potential new stars.

The studio had a small stage and a dressing area behind it. I was already wearing my tutu and pointe shoes, so I was ready for warm-ups. I had just begun when I saw Sanford wheeling Celine toward me, and an older man with a charcoal gray mustache and an older lady, tall, with her hair a tinted bluish gray and teased, walked beside them. The woman wore far too much makeup, I thought, the rouge so dark on her cheeks and the lipstick so thick on her lips it made her look like a clown.

The gentleman was in a dark blue suit and tie. He had a spry walk and a friendly smile lit by blue eyes that made him look almost as young as Sanford. The elderly lady's face was taut, her gray eyes flint cold. Even when she drew closer, she looked like someone wearing a mask.

"Janet, I want you to meet my parents, Mr. and Mrs. Westfall," Celine said.

These were the two people who would be my grandparents, I quickly thought. Before I could speak, the gentleman said, "Hello, dear."

"Hello." My voice was barely louder than a whisper.

My new grandmother gazed down at me and from head to toe I was assessed, weighed, measured.

"She is petite. Nearly thirteen, you say?" she asked Celine.

"Yes, Mother, but she moves as gracefully as a butterfly. I wouldn't want her to be any different," Celine said proudly.

"What if she doesn't grow much more?" Mrs.

Westfall asked, and as she stared down at me I noticed she was sparkling with jewelry. Around her neck she wore a dazzling diamond necklace and her fingers were covered with rings, rubies, diamonds, all in gold and platinum settings.

"Of course she'll grow," Sanford said and his indignant voice surprised me.

"I doubt it," my new grandmother muttered. "Well, where are we supposed to sit?" she said, turning and looking at the already well-filled auditorium.

"Those are our seats to the right there." Sanford nodded at some empty chairs in the first row. That appeared to please my new grandmother.

"Well, let's sit down." She headed toward the seats with a graceful gait, her head held high.

"Good luck, young lady," my new grandfather said.

"Afterward," Celine said, taking my hand, "we'll all go out for dinner and celebrate."

"Just relax and do your best," Sanford told me and gave me his special smile.

"Oh no," Celine cried when she turned in her chair. "It's my brother. Who expected he would come?"

Daniel came strutting down the aisle, a big wide grin on his face. He wore a cowboy hat, a pale yellow western shirt, jeans, and boots. Everything looked new, but because the rest of the audience was dressed as if it were really a city ballet theater, he stood out and caused an immediate wave of chatter.

"That's how you come dressed to this?" Celine said as he approached us.

"What's wrong with what I'm wearing? It cost enough," he added. "Hey, break a leg," he said to me. There wasn't a seat for him so he took a place against the wall, folded his arms, and leaned back.

Soon after Daniel arrived I left my family and joined the other performers who were at the barres exercising. Dimitri stopped and came over to me.

"Relax," he said. "You're too tight. This isn't exactly the Metropolitan Ballet, you know. It's just a bunch of proud parents mooing and gooing."

"Are your parents here?" I asked.

"Of course not," he said. "This isn't anything."

"It is to me," I admitted. He smirked. Then he smiled that arrogant smile and I was sorry that I'd let him know how important tonight was to me.

"Just pretend I'm out there with you and you'll be fine. In fact," he said leaning toward me, "imagine I'm naked."

My face instantly grew hot. He laughed and moved off to join the older students. I saw them all looking my way. He was whispering to them and they were smiling and laughing. I tried to ignore them, to concentrate on what I was doing, but my heart wouldn't stop thumping and I was having trouble catching my breath.

Finally, Madame Malisorf took the floor and the room grew so still you could hear someone clear his throat way in the back of the audience.

"Good afternoon, everyone. Thank you for

coming to our semiannual recital. We will begin today with a demonstration of some of the basic, yet difficult ballet exercises, what we call the adage portion of our class, to be performed by my primary class students. You will note how well the students maintain position and balance.

"All of them, I am happy to say, are now dancing *sur les pointes* or on pointe, as we say. As some of you who have been here before know, toe dancing was developed early in the nineteenth century but did not become widely used by ballet dancers until the eighteen thirties, when the Swedish-Italian ballerina Marie Taglioni demonstrated its potential for poetic effect. Heritage, style, technique, grace, and form are what we emphasize at the Malisorf School of Ballet.

"Without further comment, then, my primary students," she announced, did a small bow, and backed away, nodding at the piano player as she did so.

We knew what we had to do as soon as the music started and all of us took position. The most difficult part of the routine as far as I was concerned was the *entrechat,* something I had just been taught. The entrechat is one of the steps of elevation. The dancer jumps straight up, beats the calves of the legs together in midair, and lands softly. Madame Malisorf wanted us to connect that with a pirouette before coming to a graceful stop, and then a bow, hopefully to applause.

I looked at my new grandparents and then at Celine, who wore a small smile on her lips. Sanford nodded at me and gave me a wider smile.

Daniel looked like he was laughing at everyone. He stepped away from the wall and pretended to go on pointe and then fell back against the wall.

The music began. As I danced, I noticed every one of the primary students glancing at everyone else. I remembered how important it was to concentrate, to feel the music, to be in your own little world, and I tried to ignore them. The only face I caught a glimpse of was Dimitri's. He looked as sternly critical as Madame Malisorf.

The pain in my feet was excruciating. I might as well be in some sort of torture chamber, I thought. Why had Madame Malisorf been ignoring my agony? Was this really the way a dancer developed or was Dimitri right: she was pushing me because Celine wanted it that way?

Soon after we had begun, the girl beside me began to close the gap between us. Madame Malisorf never had us rehearse together. It was just assumed we would all remain in our own space and do what we were taught to do. I should have paid more attention to those around me because the girl came down after a turn and actually grazed the skirt of my tutu with her right hand.

It put me off balance, but I didn't realize it until I finished the entrechat and began to pirouette. I leaned too far in her direction so that when she turned and I spun, we collided and both lost our balance. I fell to the polished floor in an awkward flop that resulted in my sitting down hard on my hands. She continued to lose her balance and nearly collided with another dancer before falling on her side.

The audience roared with laughter, Daniel's laugh one of the loudest. Dimitri looked sick. Celine's mouth opened and closed and then her face filled with disbelief. Sanford looked sad, but my new grandmother kept shaking her head and smirking. My new grandfather just looked surprised.

Madame Malisorf, off to the right, gestured for us to rise quickly, and I did so. I started to perform the last steps again, but she shook her head and indicated I should simply stop and join the others in their bows.

There was loud applause. The guests appeared to have enjoyed our imperfections. Madame Malisorf took the center stage again and waited for silence.

"Well," she said, "that's why we spend most of our youth trying to do the simplest exercises and steps. Ballet is truly the dance of the gods," she added. "My primary students," she said gesturing at us and stressing the word *primary*. There was loud applause again and we all hurried off the stage. The older students approached to take our places. Dimitri glared at me.

My stomach felt as if it had filled with gravel. The girl who had collided with me came over to me immediately.

"You little idiot," she said. The others stopped to listen. "How could you be so clumsy? Why didn't you watch where you were going?"

"I did. You came too close to me," I cried.

"Everyone saw it. Whose fault was it?" she asked her friends.

"The Dwarf's," one of the boys quipped and they all laughed. The girl fired another look of hate at me and they walked away. I sat on a chair, my tears zigzagging down my cheeks and dropping off my chin.

"Hey, hey," I heard someone say and glanced up to see Sanford walking through the backstage area. "There's no reason for that. You did fine."

"I did horribly," I moaned.

"No, no. It wasn't your fault."

"Everyone thinks it was," I said, wiping my tears away with the back of my hands.

"Come on," he said. "We'll watch the rest of the recital."

I took his hand and went out to the audience. It seemed like everyone was looking at me and laughing. I kept my head down, my eyes fixed on my feet as we went around and down the side to reach the chairs. There were two empty ones. My new grandparents had left.

Celine said nothing. She sucked in her breath and stared at the stage as the scene from *Romeo and Juliet* began. Dimitri was as wonderful as he was in our studio. He danced as if he owned the stage and it was apparent, even to me, really just a beginner, that he made the others look better than they were. When their scene ended, the applause was louder, the faces of the guests full of appreciation. Madame Malisorf announced a reception in the next room where she would be serving hors d'oeuvres and wine for the adults.

"Let's just go home," Celine grumbled.

"Celine . . ." Sanford began and I knew he didn't want to make me feel any more awkward than I already did.

"Please," she said. "Let's just go home."

He got behind her chair and started to wheel her out. Some of the people stopped to say they enjoyed my dancing.

"Don't be discouraged, little one," a red-faced man said. "It's like riding a horse. Just get up and do it again," he advised. His wife pulled him away. Celine shot him a nasty, hateful look and then turned toward the doorway. We couldn't get out of there fast enough for her.

I wondered where Daniel was and spotted him talking to one of the older ballerinas. He waved at me as we left, but I was too embarrassed to wave back. It wasn't until we were all in the car that I spoke.

"I'm sorry, Mother," I said. "I didn't know that girl was so close to me and she didn't notice me either."

"It was the other girl's fault," Sanford comforted.

Celine was so quiet, I didn't think she would speak to me again, but after a few minutes she began.

"You can't blame anything on the other dancer. You have to be aware of the other dancer. If she or he is off, you have to compensate. That's what makes you the best." Her tone left no room for argument, but still Sanford tried to defend me.

"She's just starting, Celine," Sanford reminded her. "Mistakes are something you learn from."

"Mistakes should be made in practice, not in recital," she spat. "You'll have to work harder." She was ashamed of me and didn't pretend to hide it.

"Harder? How can she work any harder than she's working, Celine? She doesn't do anything else. She hasn't had a chance to make new friends. She needs a life, too." Sanford wouldn't give up. It shocked me since he always gave in to her so easily.

"This is her life. She wants it just as much as I want it for her. Don't you, Janet? Well?"

"Yes, Mother," I said quickly.

"See? I'll speak to Madame Malisorf. Maybe we can get her to give her one more lesson a week."

"When? On the weekend? Celine, you're being unreasonable." Sanford said.

"Sanford, I'm tired of you arguing with me. And I will not have you always taking *her* side. You are my husband, Sanford; your allegiance belongs with me. Janet *will have* an extra lesson."

Sanford shook his head.

"I still think that might be too much, Celine," Sanford said, gently this time.

"Let Madame Malisorf and I decide what's too much, Sanford."

He didn't argue anymore. As we headed for home I wondered what happened to the idea of going out to dinner? What happened to my new grandparents? I was afraid to ask, and I didn't need to since Celine told me anyway.

"My mother and father were embarrassed and went straight home," she said, her voice steely.

I didn't think it was possible to feel any smaller than I was, but I wished I could just sink into the crevices between the seats and disappear. As soon as we arrived home, I ran upstairs to my room and shut the door. A short while later, I heard a soft knock. "Come in," I called out.

Sanford entered and smiled at me. I was sitting on the bed. I had cried all the tears I had stored for sad occasions. My eyes ached.

"Now I don't want you feeling so terrible," he said kindly. "You'll have many more chances to do better."

"I'll make another mistake for sure," I said. "I'm not as good as Celine thinks I am."

"Don't underestimate yourself after just one recital, Janet. Everyone, even the greatest dancers, makes mistakes." He put his hand on my shoulder, then rubbed it along my tight, aching neck.

"She hates me now," I mumbled.

"Oh no," he said. "She's just very determined. She'll relax and realize it's not the end of the world, too. You'll see," he promised. He brushed back my hair. "You were definitely the cutest dancer out there. I'm sure most people thought you were the best one on stage," he encouraged.

"They did?"

"Sure. All eyes were on you."

"Which made it worse for me," I pointed out. He laughed.

"Now, don't you think about it anymore. Think about happy things. Isn't your real birthday next Saturday?"

"Yes, but Celine wanted to change it to the day you adopted me," I reminded him.

"That was just Celine's silly wish. Why don't you and I plan your birthday party," he said. "I know you haven't had a chance to make new friends, but maybe you'll be able to at your party. Think of some children you'd like to invite. We'll have a good time," he promised.

"Will my grandparents come?" I asked.

His smile stiffened.

"I imagine so," he said. "Now, go on. Change and we'll all have dinner."

"Celine's really not mad at me?" I asked hopefully.

"No. Celine's had a very big disappointment in her life. It's hard for her to have any more. That's all. She'll be fine. We'll all be fine," he said.

It was meant to be a promise, but it came out more like a prayer, and most of my life, my prayers had never been answered.

Ten

Madame Malisorf refused to add another day to my weekly ballet lessons. Celine and she had the conversation three days later—the very first lesson after the recital.

"No," Madame Malisorf said. "It was partly my mistake to have rushed her along. I should never have agreed to put her on pointe. I should have listened to my own instincts. Janet has to find her own level of competence, her own capabilities. Talent is like water. If you remove the obstructions, it will rise to its highest possible level by itself."

"That's not true, Madame Malisorf," Celine declared. "We must set her limits. We must determine her capabilities. She won't strive if we don't push her. She doesn't have the inner discipline."

Madame Malisorf gazed at me warming up

alongside Dimitri, who had said nothing yet about my performance at the recital.

"You must be careful. You could make her lose interest and affection for the beauty and the skills, Celine. If you overtrain an athlete, he or she starts to regress, lose muscle, skill."

"We'll take that chance. Double her training time. Money is no object," Celine insisted.

"Money has never been nor will it ever be a consideration for me," Madame Malisorf snapped back at her, holding her shoulders and head proudly.

Celine seemed to wilt in the chair.

"I know that Madame, I just meant—"

"If I am to be the girl's teacher, Celine, I am to be in control. I will determine the schedule of lessons. More is not always better. What's better is to get more quality out of what you already have. If you think otherwise—"

"Yes, yes, you're right," Celine said quickly. "Of course, you're right, Madame Malisorf. I was just so disappointed the other day and I know you were, too."

"On the contrary, I was not," she said. Celine's head lifted. Even I had to pause in my exercises and look her way.

"You weren't?" Celine sounded skeptical.

"No. I was happy to see the child get right up and attempt to continue. *That* is stamina, determination. That comes from here," she said holding her palm against her heart.

"Yes," Celine said, looking at me. "Of course,

you're right again, Madame. I'm grateful that we have you."

"Then let's not waste the time we do have, Celine." Dismissing Celine with a flick of her wrist, Madame Malisorf approached Dimitri and me and our lesson began.

It was a good lesson. Even I felt that I had accomplished more than usual. The only mention Madame Malisorf made of the recital was when she made reference to my work on pointe. For the rest of the lesson she had Dimitri take me through a series of exercises and complimented me on my work.

Yet none of this seemed to ease Celine's concerns. She sat glumly in her chair and when the lesson ended and Dimitri and Madame Malisorf were gone, Celine wheeled up to me to say she thought Madame Malisorf was wrong.

"She just doesn't want to give up her own free time," Celine said peevishly. "In ballet more is better. If you're not obsessed with it, you won't be successful. It has to be demanding on your body and your soul. I'll practice with you on the weekend," she added. "We'll begin this Saturday."

"But this Saturday is my birthday and Sanford said we're having a party. I've invited some of my classmates," I moaned.

"Oh, *Sanford* is planning your party, is he?" The look in her eyes chilled me. "Well, the party isn't an all-day affair, is it? We'll practice in the morning and you can have your party in the afternoon, if you must have it at all," she declared, then turned her chair and wheeled herself away.

Ever since the recital, Celine had been behaving differently toward me. She was more impatient, her words harsher, her eyes more critical. She spent more time alone, sometimes just sitting and staring out the window. And anytime I mentioned Sanford she narrowed her eyes and looked at me like she was trying to see inside me, see what I was thinking and feeling. Once I even found her backed into a corner, the shadows draped over her like a blanket. She was staring at the painting of herself in her dance costume.

When I mentioned my concern to Sanford, he said I should just give her time. I didn't mention that I thought Celine was upset at the time he and I spent together, though, since I was afraid he would avoid me in order to keep in Celine's good graces.

"She has her ups and downs," he explained. "Everything has been happening so fast, she just needs time to adjust."

He and I went for one of our walks on the grounds, down to the lake. It was special times like these, spending time with a daddy who loved and cared for me, that made all the hours of torture in the studio worthwhile.

"I've made all the plans for your birthday party," Sanford said when we reached the edge of the water. "We're going to have a barbecue, hot dogs and hamburgers and steaks for the adults."

"Who's coming?" I asked, hoping he would mention my new grandparents.

"Some of the people at my plant whom you've met, Mrs. Williams from Peabody, Madame Malisorf, of course, and yes," he added quickly, reading my mind, "Celine's parents and Daniel will stop by. How many people have you invited?"

"Ten," I said.

"Good. We have a nice party planned. Remember, I don't want anyone using the rowboat without an adult present, okay?"

I nodded. This was the most exciting thing in my life, even more exciting than the recital. I had never had a real birthday party. The only time I'd had a birthday cake, it was for me and two other children at the orphanage at the same time. Sharing it took away from its specialness. Birthdays aren't special without a family to help you celebrate, without a mother to remember things about your growing up and a daddy to give you that special kiss and say, "My little girl's growing up. Soon she'll have eyes for someone else beside me." Finally, I was going to have a party that really was solely my own and a big party, too!

I told Sanford that Celine wanted me to practice dance on the morning of my birthday and his eyes grew small and troubled. Later, at dinner, he mentioned it and Celine shot a look at me as if to say I had betrayed her.

"Did she go crying to you about it?" she asked. "Why is it that you've suddenly become her knight in shining armor?"

"Come on, Celine. She just mentioned it when I told her about the plans for her party. I thought we would all decorate the family room in the morning and—"

"Really, Sanford, what did you expect me to do? Climb a ladder and hang balloons?" she asked disdainfully.

"No, of course not. I just thought . . ." I could tell he was weakening.

"There are no holidays, no days off, no time to forget what is your destiny, Janet," she said, turning back to me.

"I know. I wasn't complaining," I said. I didn't want her to think I wasn't grateful.

She stared at me a moment. It was a hard look, and her eyes were full of disappointment. I had to look down at my food.

"I know you're a young girl, but as a dancer you are entering a world that requires you to become an adult faster, Janet," she continued. "It will make you stronger for everything in life. I promise."

I looked up and she smiled.

"You've come so far so fast. It wasn't long ago when you were just a lost child in that orphanage. Now you have a name and a talent. You're going to be someone. Don't give up on me," she said, her voice surprising me with its soft pleading.

"Oh, I won't do that, Mother." How could she fear that *I* would give up on *her?*

"Good. Good. Then it's settled. We'll work in the morning and then you can enjoy your party. Mildred will decorate the family room," she told Sanford.

"I'd like to help," he said.

"Yes, I suppose you would," Celine told him, and I could see her scrutinizing him as she often did me, trying to peer inside his mind.

Celine was a sterner teacher than Madame Malisorf. The morning of my birthday, she was waiting impatiently for me in the studio. I was on my way into the studio when Mildred called out to me that I had a telephone call. One of the girls at school, Betty Lowe, called to talk to me about my party and the five boys I had invited. She said everyone knew how much Josh Brown liked me. My conversation lasted longer than I realized and Celine was annoyed when I joined her in the studio, five minutes late.

"What have I told you about time and its importance when it comes to practice, Janet? I thought you understood," she snapped as soon as I entered the studio.

"I'm sorry," I said. Before I could offer any explanation, she sent me directly to the barre.

I tried but I couldn't concentrate. I couldn't help thinking about my party, about everyone getting dressed up, and about the music and the food. I just knew this party would make the kids I'd invited finally let me into their group. I didn't think I had to do anything more to impress Josh, but just in case, I would be sure to wear my prettiest dress.

As these thoughts flooded my mind, I went through the motions of my routine. Celine rolled her wheelchair over until she was only inches from me and began to criticize my form and tempo.

"You're missing your mark," she said. "No, not so fast. Listen to the music. That landing was too hard! You don't land like an elephant, you float like a butterfly. Relax your knees. No. Stop!" she screamed and covered her face with her hands.

"I'm sorry," I said when she stayed silent. "I'm trying."

"You're not trying. Your mind is elsewhere. I wish Sanford had never thought up this birthday party," she muttered, her normally pretty mouth twisted, her eyes burning with an inner rage that made me look away. "All right," she said finally. "We'll make it up later. Go get ready for your party. I know when I'm fighting a lost cause. Believe me, I know when I'm doing that," she added, still very bitter.

I apologized again, but as soon as I left her behind me in the studio and rounded the corner of the doorway, I ran through the house, up the stairs, and to my room. I wanted to try my hair in a new style and I still hadn't decided on which dress I should wear. I had decided to polish my nails, too. When my first guests arrived, I was still primping and Sanford had to come to my door to tell me it was time to come down to greet people.

The presents were piled up like Christmas gifts under a tree. Mildred had helium balloons on the ceiling with different-colored ribbons dangling. There were birthday decorations on the windows and walls, and the food was so impressive, I heard

Mrs. Williams wonder aloud what Sanford and Celine would do for a wedding.

A wedding? I thought. Would I become a famous dancer and marry another famous dancer? Would I marry a rich businessman like Sanford? Would I go to college and meet some handsome young man? It was as if my life here was the key to unlocking a treasure chest of fantasies, fantasies that could actually come true!

My new grandparents were the last to arrive. I heard Celine ask about Daniel and saw her mother grimace.

"Who knows where he is?" she groaned. "That's why we're late. He was supposed to drive us."

"Happy birthday," my grandfather said when he saw me standing nearby. He was the one who handed me my present.

"Yes, happy birthday," my grandmother followed. She didn't give me much more than a passing glance before getting into a conversation with the other guests. My grandfather began a discussion with Sanford and I returned to my friends. We danced and drank punch and ate. Josh was at my side most of the time, although suddenly Billy Ross was asking me to dance as well.

Afterward, I cut the huge birthday cake. I had to blow out the candles and everyone sang "Happy Birthday" to me, everyone but my grandmother, who stood staring with a dark, unhappy expression on her face. While we ate cake I opened presents and everyone oohed and ahed over the pretty clothes, the hair dryer, the jewelry. My grandparents had bought me a pair of leather gloves that turned out to be at least two sizes too big.

I hated to see the party come to an end. Josh stayed behind and reminded me I had promised to show him our lake. I told Sanford where we were going and we left the house. It was a bit cool and overcast. I wore my new leather jacket that Sanford and Celine had bought me.

"This is a great house," Josh said. "It's twice as big as mine. And all this land, I could have my own baseball field," he continued. "You're lucky."

"I am lucky," I said. We stood at the crest of the hill, looking down at the lake.

"I'm glad you transferred into our school," Josh said. "Otherwise, I probably wouldn't have ever met you."

"No, you wouldn't have," I said, thinking about where I had come from. I was almost tempted to tell him the truth. He was so sweet, but I was afraid that the moment he heard the word *orphan,* he would back away and pretend he never knew me.

"Can we go in the rowboat?" he asked when he spotted the boat docked onshore.

"My father doesn't want me to go without an adult. I don't swim," I confessed.

"Really? How come?"

I shrugged.

"I just never learned."

His eyes grew narrow and his eyebrows nearly touched. Then he smiled.

"Maybe I'll be the one to teach you this summer."

"I'd like that," I said.

"I never gave you a birthday kiss," he said.

I didn't move and he leaned toward me slowly. I closed my eyes and there, on the crest of the hill behind my new home, I was kissed for the first time on the lips. It didn't last long. There was even a little friction shock, but I thought it was the most wonderful kiss in the world, better than any I had seen on television or in the movies. The little warm feeling that followed lingered for a moment around my heart and then trickled into my pool of memories where it would stay forever and ever.

"Janet!" We turned to see Sanford beckoning. "Josh's father is here to pick him up."

"Okay," I called back and we started for the house. Josh took my hand. Neither of us spoke. We let go before we rounded the house to greet his father, who wished me a happy birthday.

"See you in school," Josh said. I wished I could kiss him good-bye, but he looked embarrassed and hurried to get into his father's car. Moments later, he was waving good-bye and my party was over. I felt like I did when we were given some wonderful special dessert at the orphanage. When it was coming to an end, I wanted to linger and linger over the last tidbits of pleasure.

I went back inside. Mildred was busy cleaning up, but she didn't look upset about the extra work and when I offered to help her, she laughed and said not to worry. I was about to go upstairs to change out of my party dress, when I heard voices in the dining room. My grandparents were still here, having coffee and talking with Celine.

I was nervous about interrupting them, so I hesitated near the door. Just before I decided I would enter and try to get to know them a little better, I heard my grandmother say, "She'll always be a stranger to me, Celine. She's not of our blood and blood is the most important thing in a family."

"That's ridiculous, Mother, and anyway, I'm not concerned about family. I don't just want a daughter. Anyone can have a daughter. I want a dancer." My heart fell at her words. What did she mean?

"More reason to question what you are doing, Celine. I saw the girl at the recital. What in heaven's name caused you to believe she had anything special?"

"She does," Celine insisted.

"Well, if she does, she keeps it well hidden," my grandmother said. "Where is she? You would think she would show some respect. I took the time to come here."

I decided that was my cue and I entered.

"Hello," I said, my voice quavering, my stomach in knots over Celine's words. "Thank you for the present, Grandmother and Grandfather." My grandfather nodded and smiled. My grandmother tightened the corner of her mouth.

"We have to go," she said. "Your brother is a constant worry for me," she added, looking at Celine. "I'm afraid he's going to end up marrying one of those floozies and disgrace all of us one of these days," she added as she rose.

"It's your own fault," Celine said. "You spoiled him."

"I didn't spoil him. Your father spoiled him," she accused.

"He'll be all right," Sanford said. "He's just sowing his wild oats."

"Really?" my grandmother said. "Well, when do you think he'll run out of oats?"

Sanford laughed and then escorted them out. My grandfather patted me on the head as they left and mumbled something about "Many happy returns."

I remained with Celine, who sat there brooding in her chair.

"Thank you for the party," I told her. She looked up as if just realizing I was still in the room.

"Where were you?"

"I went for a walk with Josh to show him the lake," I said.

She rolled her chair around the table and came toward me.

"You've got to be careful when it comes to boys," she began.

I smiled. I was just thirteen.

"I know what you're thinking. You think you have plenty of time to worry about romance, but believe me, you don't. Not you. You're special. I don't want you to turn your brain into Jell-O with silly lovesickness. It's distracting and this morning you saw what distraction can do."

She drew closer until we were gazing into each other's eyes.

"Sex draws on your creative energies, Janet. It can drain you," she explained. "When I was dancing and approaching the peak of my development, I refrained from all sexual activities with Sanford. For a long time, we even slept in separate rooms," she added.

I didn't say anything and I didn't move. I don't think I even blinked.

"I had many boys chasing after me, especially when I was your age," she continued, "but I didn't have time to waste on schoolgirl crushes. You won't either so don't encourage any." She started to wheel herself away and stopped. "Tomorrow," she said, "we'll try to make up for today."

She left me standing there looking after her. "Make up for today?" She made it sound as if my birthday and my birthday party were a total inconvenience.

I had a grandmother who didn't really want me and a mother who only wanted me so that I could be the dancer she couldn't be.

No, Josh, I thought, maybe I'm not as lucky as you imagine.

Outside, the sky turned darker. The rain began and the drops that hit the windows looked like heaven's tears.

Eleven

Once Celine and I began working weekends on my dancing, it became a regular part of my schedule. A number of times, Sanford tried to plan family outings: day trips, shopping, movie matinees, or just a ride and dinner in a nice restaurant. Celine not only rejected his suggestions; she became annoyed and angry at him just for making them.

After my birthday party, I was invited to other girls' houses, and one night I was invited to a pajama party at Betty Lowe's. Celine always had a reason why I shouldn't go, the primary one being I would stay up too late, be too tired, and start my dance practice too late.

"Parents don't watch their children very well anymore," she told me. "I can't be sure you'll be well chaperoned, and I know what happens at these all-girl parties. Boys always sneak over and then . . . things happen. Not that I ever went to any sleepovers—I knew enough not to be distracted," she added.

I tried to explain my situation to my new friends, but after I had turned down half a dozen invitations, the invitations stopped coming and once again, I felt a gap growing between me and the other students at the school. Even Josh began to lose interest in me because we never had a chance to be alone. Once, and only because Sanford had talked Celine into permitting me to go with him to the factory after my dance lesson on a Saturday, I was able to meet Josh at the custard stand. Sanford knew that was why I wanted to go along with him and he permitted me to stay there for nearly two hours before coming around to bring me home.

"It's probably best for you not to mention this to Celine," Sanford told me. "Not that we want to keep any secrets from her. I just don't want her worrying."

I nodded, but he didn't have to ask. I wouldn't have dreamed of mentioning it.

I did my best to explain my situation to Josh, but he couldn't understand how my dancing prevented me from doing nearly everything any of the other kids could do. The crisis came when he formally asked me to the movies. His father was going to drive us. Sanford said yes but Celine said no and they got into the worst argument they had since I had arrived.

"This time it's only a night at the movies and ice cream afterward, ice cream full of fat that she doesn't need. Tomorrow it will be a whole week-end day and night. And then she'll be wanting to go on weekend jaunts with girls who have nothing but bubble gum brains and two left feet."

"She's only thirteen, Celine."

"When I was thirteen, I had performed in twelve programs and I had danced in *Sleeping Beauty* at the Albany Center for the Performing Arts. You've seen the news clippings."

"That's you. Janet's Janet."

"Janet has opportunities now she would never have had, Sanford. It's practically sinful to do anything that would frustrate or detract from them." She would not be dissuaded.

"But—"

"Haven't you done enough damage to ballet for one lifetime?" she screamed at him.

When Sanford came to my door that evening, I already knew what the decision was.

"I'm sorry," he said. "Celine thinks you're too young for this sort of thing."

He said it with his head down, his eyes on the floor.

"I'll think of something nice for us to do soon," he added, and left me crying tears into my pillow.

Josh's face dropped and actually turned ashen when I told him I couldn't go with him that Friday night. I tried to give him an explanation, but he just shook his head.

"What is it, your parents don't think I'm rich enough?" he shot back at me and then turned and left me standing alone in the school hallway before I could deny it.

I felt as if I were entering Celine's private world of shadows now. One of my girlfriends called to tease me and sang, "All work and no play make Janet a dull girl." The world that had become filled with sunshine and color began to turn shades of gray. Even when it was a clear sky, I felt as if clouds hung over me. My moodiness seeped into my performances at lessons. Madame Malisorf's eyes narrowed into slits of suspicion. Celine had made me promise never to tell Madame Malisorf how hard she and I worked on the weekends, but my master teacher was too perceptive.

"Aren't you resting your legs?" she asked me directly one afternoon. Celine was in her usual corner observing. I glanced her way. Madame Malisorf followed the shift in my eyes and turned.

"Celine, are you working this student seven days a week?" she demanded.

"On occasion, I go over something with her, Madame Malisorf. She's young and—"

"I want her to have a full twenty-four hours of rest. Those muscles need some time to rebuild. Every time we work out, we break them down. You, of all people, should know that," she said, shaking her head. "Make sure she has the rest required," she demanded.

Celine promised, but never kept her promise, and if I mentioned it, she would go into a rage and then a depression, backing herself into one of those dark corners in the house to stare sadly at the pictures of her former self. Sometimes, she simply read and reread a dance program and I'd find her asleep in her chair, the program in her lap, clutched tightly in her fingers. I didn't have the heart to put up any real resistance.

I tried to do better, to be sharp, to hit my marks. Now, without any friends calling me, I did my homework and went to bed early. I even did what she had asked me to do when I first enrolled in school. I pretended to have cramps and got myself excused from physical education class a number of times. I needed to conserve my energy. I had grown terrified of being tired or sluggish.

Summer was drawing closer and with it was the promise of attending a prestigious dance school. However, money couldn't buy someone a place in the school. Everyone had to audition and Celine's new obsession was getting me prepared for that audition. Madame Malisorf agreed to help win me a spot. She thought it was a good idea for me to go to the school because she was going to spend most of her summer in Europe as she usually did. My lessons became reviews of fundamentals. Dimitri rarely came to practice anymore. He had already been accepted to a school for dance in New York City and was preparing himself for the new training.

We had to travel to Bennington, Vermont, where the audition for the dance school was being held. I was actually excited about it because I would be spending eight weeks at the school and I had read the program and schedule and seen that there was more rest and recreation time than I now had. Of course, almost anywhere would give me more time. At the end of the school's brochure were testimonials written by former students and many of them talked about the social events, singing around the campfire, their weekly social dance, and short bus trips to museums and historic sights. Not everything had to do with dance. The school's philosophy was that a more rounded person makes a more complete artist. It was very expensive to go there and it amazed me that so many people would compete to spend so much money.

At my final lesson before the audition, Madame Malisorf put me through what she predicted would be the school's test. She stood back alongside Celine and tried to be an objective judge. At the end she and Celine spoke softly for a moment and then Madame Malisorf smiled.

"I would give you a place in my school, Janet," she said. "You've made considerable improvement and you have reached a quality of performance that would justify the investment of further time and effort," she claimed. Celine beamed.

I was happy too because I really wanted to get into the school. I think a part of me, a strong part of me, wanted to get away for a while, and not feel so guilty about every misstep. Before she left, Madame Malisorf warned Celine not to wear me out.

"She's a fragile commodity now, Celine. We've taken her far, too far too fast perhaps, but she's there. Now let's let her develop at a normal pace.

Otherwise . . ." She looked at me. "We'll ruin what we've created."

"Don't worry, Madame. I will cherish her as much as I cherished myself, if not more."

Despite the hard days and the difficult lessons, despite her critical eyes and often harsh comments, I had grown to appreciate and respect Madame Malisorf. I was even a bit afraid of what would happen without her overseeing everything, but she left assuring me that my teachers at the school would be of the highest quality.

"I'll see you in September," she told me and left.

"I knew it," Celine declared once we were alone. "I knew she would come to see you as I do. We must continue to prepare. This is wonderful, wonderful," she said and for the next few days, she was as animated and excited as she had been when I first arrived.

Sanford, however, looked more troubled by it all. Problems at the factory took up more and more of his time and he continually apologized to me about it. It was as if he was sorry he was leaving me alone with Celine so much. Celine wasn't the least bit interested in the factory and didn't have the patience to listen to anything Sanford said. She was so focused on my audition, it seemed that she thought of nothing else from the moment she rose to the moment she fell asleep.

And then, the week before my audition, there was a new family crisis. Daniel had run off and married a woman he had gotten pregnant. My grandparents were overwrought. They held a family meeting at our house. I wasn't invited, but they spoke so loudly, I would have had to have been deaf not to hear.

"Both my children just go out and do impulsive things," Grandmother cried. "Neither of you thinks about the family name anymore."

I heard them all trying to calm her, but she was beside herself. They talked about Daniel's new wife and how she came from a lower class of people.

"What sort of a child would a woman like that produce?" Grandmother asked. "We should disown them both. We should."

If they did that, what would happen to the baby? I wondered. Would he or she become an orphan like I was?

The sound of discussion turned to the sounds of sobbing. Soon afterward, my grandparents emerged, my grandmother looking distraught, her eyes bloodshot, her makeup smudged. She gazed at me, then turned and hurried out of the house.

Daniel was the main subject of conversation at the beginning of dinner that night, but Celine put a quick, sharp end to it.

"I don't want to hear his name anymore this week. I don't want anything to distract us from our objective, Sanford. Forget about him."

"But your parents . . ." he began.

"They'll get over it," she said, and turned to me to talk about the things we should sharpen in my presentation.

Finally, the day arrived. I had trouble sleeping the night before, slipping in and out of nightmares. In most I either fell or got so dizzy in my pirouette, I looked clumsy. I saw heads shaking and Celine shrinking in her wheelchair.

The moment I moved my legs to get out of bed that morning, I felt the pain in my stomach. It was as if there was a fist closing inside me and then my lower back ached so hard and deeply, it brought tears to my eyes. I crunched up and took deep breaths. The warm trickle on the inside of my thigh sent chills of terror shooting down to my feet and bouncing back up through my body to curl in my head and make my brain scream. Gingerly, inches at a time, I reached down, and when I saw the blood on my fingertips, I cried.

"No, not now, not today," I pleaded with my insistent body.

I swung my legs around, but when I put my weight on them, they crumbled and I found myself on all fours, the pain growing worse, nearly taking my breath away. I went on my side and lay there in a fetal position, trying to catch my breath. That was when my door burst open and Celine wheeled herself in, her face full of excitement as she cried, "Wake up, wake up. Today is our day. Wake . . ."

She froze, her hands glued to the top of her wheels as she stared down at me.

"What are you doing, Janet?"

"It's . . . my period, Mother," I said. "I woke up and I was bleeding. I have such cramps and my back aches. I have a terrible headache, too. Every time I lift my head a little, it feels like steel marbles are rolling around inside me."

"Why didn't you put on the protection I bought you?" she demanded. "You should always be anticipating this. I told you," she insisted when I shook my head.

"No, you never told me to do that before I went to sleep every night."

"This is ridiculous. Get up on your feet. Clean yourself and get dressed. I'll have Mildred change the sheets on your bed. Get up!" she screamed.

I heard Sanford pounding his feet on the steps as he charged up our stairway.

"What is it, Celine? Why are you shouting? What's wrong?" he cried and came through the doorway, stopping just behind her. "Janet!"

"It's nothing. She's only gotten her period."

"It hurts so much," I wailed.

"Don't be ridiculous," Celine insisted.

"If she says it hurts, Celine . . ." Sanford began.

"Of course it hurts, Sanford. It's never pleasant, but she's just being melodramatic."

"I don't know. I've heard of young girls practically being incapacitated. My sister had to be brought home from school. I remember—"

"Your sister is an idiot," Celine said and wheeled herself closer to me. "Get up this minute," she ordered.

I struggled into a sitting position and then, using the bed, started to rise. Sanford rushed to my side and helped me stand.

"You're going to ruin the rug. Get into the

bathroom. Don't you have any pride?" Celine screamed.

"Stop yelling at her," Sanford urged. He helped me into the bathroom and then stepped out while I cleaned myself and found the sanitary napkins. I had to sit on the closed toilet seat to catch my breath. The pain didn't lessen.

"What are you doing in there?" Celine called. She came to the bathroom door.

I reached for the sink and pulled myself up. Every step brought more pain. I opened the door and looked out at her.

"It hurts so much," I complained.

"It will go away. Get dressed. We're leaving in an hour," she said and spun around.

I started out of the bathroom. The cramps kept me clutching my stomach and leaning over. I tried to move around the room, get my dress from the closet, put on my shoes, but the pain just got worse. The only position that brought any relief was lying on my side and pulling my legs up.

How would I ever dance today? I wondered. How could I perform those leaps and turns? Just the thought of going on pointe brought more pain to my back and stomach. My head was pounding.

"What are you doing?" I heard Celine cry. She was in my doorway. "Why aren't you dressed?"

I didn't reply. I clutched my stomach and took deep breaths.

"Janet!"

"What's happening now?" Sanford asked.

"She's not getting dressed. Look at her," Celine demanded.

"Janet," Sanford said. "Are you all right?"

"No," I groaned. "Every time I try to stand, it hurts."

"She can't possibly go today, Celine. You'll have to postpone it," he told her.

"Are you mad? You can't postpone this. There are so many girls trying out. They'll choose their quota before she has a chance to compete. We've got to go," Celine insisted.

"But she can't even stand," he protested.

"Of course she can. Stand up," Celine ordered. She wheeled toward the bed. Sanford held out his hands to stop her.

"Celine, please."

"Stand up, stand up, you ungrateful urchin. Stand up!" she screamed at the top of her lungs.

I had to try again. I rose and put my feet down. Sanford stood and watched as I made the effort. As my body straightened, the pain in my stomach shot up into my chest. I cried, folded, and fell back to the bed.

"Stand up!" Celine shouted.

Sanford forcefully turned her around in the chair.

"Stop this. She has to go. Stop it, Sanford. Stop it," she cried. He continued to wheel her forcefully out of my room.

"She probably needs some kind of medication. I'll have to take her to the doctor," he said.

"That's ridiculous. You fool. She won't get into the school. Janet!" she cried, her voice echoing in the hallway.

My body tightened. I was so frightened. I

squeezed my eyes shut to clamp out the world around me. There was a buzzing in my ear and then a darkness, a comfortable, easeful darkness in which I no longer felt the pain and the agony.

I felt like I was floating. My arms had turned into paper-thin wings. I was drifting through the darkness toward a pinhole of light and it felt so wonderful, so easy. I glided and turned, dove and rose, fluttering.

Then I passed what looked like a wall of mirrors on both sides, drifting, gently raising and lowering my paper-thin wings. I looked at myself as I continued toward the light.

And amazingly, I was a butterfly.

Twelve

"**W**hat's wrong with her?" I heard a voice say. It sounded far away, like a voice at the end of a tunnel, so it was hard to recognize it.

"All of her vital signs are good. This is some sort of anxiety attack, Sanford."

"That's ridiculous," another voice snapped. The darkness began to diminish a bit. "She has nothing to make her anxious. She has more than most girls her age have."

"You don't know as much about her past as you think you do, Celine. There are many things working in the subconscious mind. And then this might all be due to the psychological trauma of having her first period," he added.

"Did you ever hear anything so ridiculous as that? Please, Doctor," Celine insisted. "Give her something."

"There's nothing to give her but a little time and then a lot of tender loving care, Celine."

"What do you think she's been getting?"

"Celine." Sanford's strong voice broke through the darkness.

"Well, he talks like we've been torturing the child," she said.

The darkness dwindled some more and the light began to grow stronger, wider. My eyelids fluttered.

"She's waking up."

I opened my eyes and looked into Dr. Franklin's face.

"Hello there," he said, smiling. "How are you doing?"

I was so confused. I closed my eyes and tried to think and then I opened them and looked around. I was still in my room. Celine was at the foot of my bed and Sanford was standing beside her with his hand on the back of her chair.

"Can you sit up?" the doctor asked.

I nodded and started to do so. I was a little dizzy, but that passed quickly and I was up. There was a dull ache in my back and my stomach felt woozy. I gazed at the clock and saw that it was midafternoon.

"There. She'll be fine," the doctor said. "Just a day's rest now. The worst is over," he added.

"Is it?" Celine asked dryly. She was shaking her head and glaring at me.

The doctor closed his bag and left the room with Sanford. Celine wheeled herself closer.

"I don't know what happened to me, Mother," I said. "I'll get dressed."

"Dressed?" She laughed a thin, bone-chilling laugh. "For what? It's over. Your chance to get into the school is over. We missed the audition."

"Can't we reschedule it?" I asked. My throat was so dry, it hurt to speak.

"No. There's no point in it," she said, her eyes small. "They went through dozens of girls and filled their openings by now."

"I'm sorry," I said.

"Me too. All this work, the hours and hours of lessons, the best shoes . . ." She shook her head, turned her chair, and wheeled out of my room.

I stepped off the bed and started for the bathroom. It felt like I was walking on a floor of balloons. My ankles wobbled at first and then I grew stronger. I splashed cold water on my face and brushed back my hair. Still feeling weak, I went to my closet and found something to wear. Mildred came to my room just as I finished dressing.

"Mr. Delorice wanted me to see if you were hungry," she said. "I'll bring you something."

"No, I can come down. Thank you, Mildred."

She said she would make me some hot soup and a toasted cheese sandwich, which I told her sounded good. When I went out into the hallway I saw the door to Celine's bedroom was open so I peeked in. She was in bed, staring up at the ceiling.

"I'm feeling better," I said. She didn't respond. "Are you all right, Mother?"

She closed her eyes. My heart began to thump. Was she so angry at me that she would pretend not to hear me? I hurried away as fast as I could and descended the stairs. Sanford was on the phone in his den talking to someone at his factory. He waved when I appeared in the doorway and indicated he would be right with me. I went into the dining room and Mildred brought me my soup and sandwich.

"Is Celine very angry at me?" I asked when Sanford appeared.

"No, no," he said. "She's disappointed, but things will look better in the morning. They always do. How are you doing?" he asked, petting my hair.

"I'm better. I feel like I just climbed a high mountain and ran miles," I told him. He smiled and nodded.

"I guess it's true when they say men have it easier. I'll just go look in on Celine," he added and left to go upstairs.

When he came down again, he looked more concerned. He flashed a quick smile at me and told me he had to go to the factory for a little while.

"Celine's resting. Try not to disturb her," he added, and left.

I went upstairs quietly, thinking again that I would just peek in on her, but Celine's door was closed. It remained closed for the rest of the day and night. I watched some television, read, and went up to bed before Sanford returned from the factory.

When I woke in the morning, I did feel better. The sun was shining brightly through my curtains. I wanted to wear something cheerful so I chose a yellow blouse with a white skirt and the light blue sneakers Celine and Sanford had bought me the first week I arrived. I fixed my hair into a ponytail. When I stepped out of my room, I saw that Celine's bedroom door was still closed, but I imagined Sanford was downstairs at the dining room table, reading his paper and waiting for me as he had been almost every morning since they brought me here from the orphanage.

When I got downstairs, however, there was no one in the dining room. Mildred came from the kitchen and told me Sanford had been up very early and was already gone.

"What about my mother?" I asked her.

"I brought her breakfast, but she didn't eat much of her dinner last night and she didn't look like she was very interested in any breakfast. She hardly spoke," she added, shaking her head. "I think she's sick."

"Maybe Sanford went for the doctor," I said.

"No," Mildred said. The way she pressed her lips shut told me she knew more. "He didn't go for the doctor."

"What is it, Mildred? What else is wrong?"

"I don't know that anything's wrong," she said. "Mr. Delorice, he was very concerned about his business this morning. Not that I listen in on his phone calls," she added quickly.

"I know you don't, Mildred. Please tell me what you do know," I pleaded.

"Something happened at the factory this week, but I don't know what. I just know it's made him very upset," she said. "I'll bring you some breakfast."

"I'm going up to see my mother first," I told her and hurried up the stairway. I knocked on Celine's door but she didn't respond. I waited a moment and then opened it slowly and peered in.

Celine was in her wheelchair staring out a window. She was still in her nightgown and her hair was unbrushed. She wore no lipstick.

"Mother?" I said coming up behind her. She didn't turn, so I spoke louder. She simply stared out the window. "Are you all right, Mother?"

Suddenly she started to laugh. It began with a low rumbling in her throat, and then her face broke into a wide smile with a wild look in her eyes and her laughter got louder, stranger. Tears began to stream out of her eyes. Her shoulders shook. She seized the wheels of her chair and rolled them forward and then backward, and forward again until she hit the wall.

"Mother, what are you doing? Why are you doing that?" I cried.

She simply laughed and continued.

I stepped away.

"Stop it," I screamed. "Please."

Her laughter grew even louder as she wheeled forward and backward, each time slamming harder into the wall.

"Mother! Stop!"

She didn't so I turned and ran from the room

right into Sanford, who was coming up the stairway.

"Something's wrong with Celine," I cried. "She won't stop laughing and she keeps wheeling her chair into the wall."

"What? Oh no."

He hurried past me and into the bedroom. I heard him pleading with her to stop. Her laughter was still so loud I had to cover my ears because it was so terrifying. Mildred came to the foot of the stairway.

"What's wrong, Janet?"

"It's Celine. She won't stop laughing."

"Oh no," she said and shook her head. "She did that once before." She shook her head again and walked away.

I looked toward Celine's bedroom, my heart thumping so hard I thought my chest would just split apart.

Finally the laughter stopped. I started toward the bedroom but before I got there, Sanford closed the door. I stood there for a while and then went downstairs to wait. Mildred brought me some juice, toast, and eggs, but I couldn't eat anything. Not long afterward, I heard the doorbell and Mildred welcomed Dr. Franklin. He hurried up the stairs. I followed, but again I heard the bedroom door shut.

The doctor remained in there a long time. I went downstairs to wait and then went out front and sat on the bench under the weeping willow trees. It was such a pretty day, with only a puff of marshmallow cloud here and there. Birds were singing and fluttering all around me. A curious squirrel paused and stared at me, even when I began to speak to it. Then it scurried up a tree. On such a glorious morning, how could things be so gray and dismal in my heart?

Finally the front door opened. Sanford stood talking softly to Dr. Franklin for a few moments. They shook hands and the doctor walked to his car. I rose and he looked my way.

"And how are you feeling?" he asked.

"I'm better. How's my mother?"

"Sanford will speak to you," he said cryptically and got into his car. I watched him drive off and then I hurried into the house. Sanford was in his den on the phone again. He held his right forefinger up and then turned in his chair so his back was to me as he continued his conversation. I didn't know where to go. Suddenly I felt so lost. I felt like a stranger, an intruder. Celine's bedroom door was still shut tight. I wandered through the house, paused at the studio, and then went up to my room and sat on my bed, waiting. It seemed forever until Sanford came up.

"I'm sorry," he said. "I have a crisis at my plant. It seems my foreman was embezzling from me but luckily I found out in time. I could have been bankrupted. I've had to work things out with my business manager and accountant as well as the district attorney and that's still not over. In the middle of it all . . . well, Celine's not doing well."

"What's wrong with her?" I asked, my eyes tearing. "Is it all my fault?"

"No, no," he said. He stood there gazing at me for a moment and then he took a deep breath, looked toward the window, his own eyes glassing over, and shook his head. "It's all my fault. I put her in that chair, not you. I took away the thing that meant the most to her, that gave her a reason to be. We've just been going through the motions of living ever since," he added. "Then, she woke up one morning and thought about us adopting someone like you. I thought it was our salvation, my salvation, I should say.

"I didn't think it out properly," he continued, crossing my room to stand by the window. He spoke with his back to me. "I should have realized what you, what anyone in your shoes—pointe shoes," he corrected, turning to me with a smile, "would be put through. It wasn't fair."

"I didn't mind it," I said quickly. "It's been hard, but . . ."

"It's been cruel," he corrected, turning to me. "That's what it's been. Your childhood has been disregarded, ignored, sacrificed to satisfy an unrealistic dream. You can never be what Celine wants—you can't give her back her legs, her career, her dream. No one can, even the most talented dancer. She tried to live through you, and I am sorry to say, I let it happen because it bought me some peace and relief from my own dark, oppressive clouds of guilt." He smiled. "In a way, Janet, I have been exploiting you, too. I'm sorry."

"I don't understand," I cried.

"I know. It's too much to lay on someone your

age. It's very unfair to burden you so. This family has more baggage than anyone can imagine.

"Anyway," he continued with his hands behind his back, "I can't ignore Celine's deeper problems anymore. She's going to need professional help and it will be a very long and arduous journey, one that may never end. I'm sorry," he said, "that I ever permitted you to be brought into this. You're still young enough to have another chance, a better chance for a good, healthy young life."

"What do you mean?" I asked, my heart stopping.

"I can't take care of Celine and give you the proper home life you deserve at the same time," he said. "It's better for everyone if you have another opportunity."

"Another opportunity?" He couldn't be saying what I thought he was.

"It won't be pleasant for you here, Janet, and I don't think Celine will make any improvements if she sees you and believes she's failed again. Not that I think she has. I think you've done splendidly, and anyone in a normal family situation would be proud of you. I'm proud of you. I am. But I'm also very afraid for you.

"The truth is," he said, gazing toward the window again, "I'm even afraid for myself."

He smiled at me. It was a brave smile.

"I hate to lose you. You're a delightful young lady and a pleasure to have around. This place is not going to be the same," he said. "I want you to know you mean a lot to me, Janet. You brought some real light into my life and into our home. Now it's my turn to bring light into yours."

"You're giving me back?" I finally asked, choking back the tears.

"I don't want to, but that's what's best. I've got to devote all my time to getting Celine well. I owe her that, Janet, surely you understand. There won't be anyone to look after you properly and I'm afraid Celine won't be any sort of mother to anyone.

"You've already seen what your grandparents are like. They're absorbed now in their own little crisis with Daniel. I swear he does what he does just to torment them. No," Sanford said, "this is not a happy little family at the moment and certainly no place in which to nurture a child. You deserve better."

"It's all my fault," I cried. "Because I got my period at the worst time."

"No, no, no," Sanford cajoled. "I see now that it was a blessing. I mean, just suppose you went to that audition and weren't chosen. She would have had the same reaction, and if you were chosen, you would have some other test in due time, a test that you wouldn't pass to her satisfaction. You never could because you can't be her. I think she's realized that; she's facing it and that's why she's . . . having her problems. The truth is, Janet, Celine may have to be institutionalized. This is so painful for me. I'm sorry," he said. "Please, don't blame yourself. I'll see to what has to be done. I'm sure that it won't be long before another, healthier, couple scoops you up."

He kissed me on the forehead and left. I sat there, stunned, gazing around my beautiful room. Just as fast as it had been given to me, it was going to be taken away. I wished I had never been brought here, I thought. It was worse to have seen this and lost it than never to have seen it at all. How many mommies and daddies would I lose? How many times would I have to say good-bye?

I was angry, raging inside, my emotions tossing and turning like waves in a hurricane. I felt betrayed. I was never really given the chance to love them.

At dinner Sanford told me he had made arrangements and that the child protection service wanted me to go to a group foster home where I would stay until I was adopted again.

"They said it was very nice and you would have lots of new friends."

"I made lots of new friends here," I said.

He nodded, his eyes sad.

"I'm sorry, Janet. It breaks my heart. It really does," he said and turned away, but not before I saw the tears in his eyes.

I believed him, but it didn't make any of it easier. In fact, it made it harder.

There was a flurry of activity the following morning. A special-duty nurse arrived to help with Celine, and soon after, the Westfalls visited. Celine's mother gave me little more than a passing glance before she went upstairs to see Celine. Afterward, Sanford and his father-in-law went into Sanford's office to discuss the events at the glass factory. When they were leaving, my grandmother looked in at me in the living room, turned to Sanford, and said, "Celine wasted precious energy to make a silk purse out of a sow's ear."

I wasn't sure what it all meant, but I sensed that she was blaming me.

Later in the day, Sanford sent Mildred up to my room to help me pack my things. I still had not seen Celine because she hadn't come out of her room and her door was always shut, but I couldn't leave without at least speaking to her one more time. I went to the door and knocked. The nurse opened it.

"I have to say good-bye," I told her. She wasn't going to let me in, but Sanford had come up for me and told her it was okay. She stepped aside and I entered.

Celine was in her wheelchair at the window, just gazing out at the front yard. I put my hand on hers and she turned very slowly.

"I'm sorry, Celine. I wanted you to be my mother. I wanted to dance for you."

She simply stared at me as if I were a total stranger.

"I hope you get better real soon. Thank you for trying to make me a prima ballerina."

She blinked.

"It's time," Sanford said from the doorway.

I nodded, leaned over, and kissed Celine on the cheek.

"Good-bye," I whispered.

As I turned, she seized my hand.

"Are there a lot of people out there? Is it a big audience?" she asked.

"What?"

She smiled.

"I'm just warming up. Tell Madame Malisorf I'll be right there and tell her I'm ready. Tell her I've already begun to hear the music. She likes that. Will you tell her?"

"Yes, Celine, of course." I had no idea what she was talking about.

"Thank you," she said and turned back to the window.

For a moment I thought I did hear the music. I remembered what she had told me when we had first met. "When you're good, and you will be good, you will lose yourself in the music, Janet. It will carry you off. . . ."

It was carrying me off now.

I looked back at her once and then left her home forever.

Epilogue

When we drove away from the house, I did not look back. I felt as if I was leaving a storybook and the covers were being closed behind me. I didn't want to see my story end. I wanted to remember it forever as it was: bright, warm, full of the magic of flowers and birds, rabbits and squirrels, a fantasy house, my land of Oz.

I sat in the rear of the big car. In the trunk were two suitcases full of my new clothes, shoes, and ballet costumes, as well as my wonderful pointe shoes. At first I didn't want to take anything. I wanted to leave with little more than I had when I had arrived. Then I thought, if I didn't have these things, I would surely wake up one morning and think I had dreamed it all, all the faces, all the voices, even my birthday party.

"I hope you'll keep up with your dancing," Sanford said. "You really were getting very good."

I didn't say anything. I sat quietly and gazed out the side window watching the scenery drift by. It felt as if the world were on a ribbon that unraveled and floated behind us. Every once in a while, Sanford would say something else. I saw him gazing at me in the rearview mirror. His eyes were full of sadness and guilt.

"I hope Celine gets better," I told him.

"Thank you." And again I saw tears in his eyes.

We were going to the group foster home, a place called The Lakewood House. Sanford explained that it was run by a couple, Gordon and Louise Tooey, who used to run it as a tourist rooming house. It was a little under a two-hour drive.

"It will only be temporary for you, I'm sure," he said.

On the way he wanted to stop to get me something to eat, but I told him I wasn't hungry. The faster we got there and I started my new life, the better, I thought. At the moment I truly felt in limbo.

Sanford followed written directions but he got lost once and had to pull into a garage for new directions. Finally we were on the road that led to the group house.

"There it is," Sanford declared.

Ahead of us was a very large, gray two-story house. It had as much if not more grounds than Sanford and Celine's home. I saw four young girls walking together toward what looked like a ball field. Two teenage boys were mowing grass and a tall, muscular man with a shock of dark brown hair and a chiseled face was shouting at some other children who were raking up the cut grass.

"Looks nice," Sanford commented.

After we parked he got out my suitcases. A tall brunette with shoulder-length hair pinned back burst out of the front entrance. She looked about fifty and I thought her best feature was her startling blue eyes.

"This must be Janet. I've been expecting you all day, sweetheart," she declared, coming right up to me. "What a pretty little girl you are."

"Yes, she is," Sanford said sadly.

"Welcome to The Lakewood House, honey. My name is Louise. I'll show you to your room. Right now, she has a room all to herself," she told Sanford, "but we're expecting new children soon."

He smiled and nodded.

"Gordon!" Louise shouted. "Gordon."

"What is it?" he called back.

"The new girl's arrived."

"Wonderful. I gotta look after these kids, they never get the lawn right," he said. He looked very grouchy to me.

"Gordon takes pride in how we keep up the place," Louise explained. "All of us help, but you'll see. It's fun," she said. "Come on in. Please," she added, putting her hand on my shoulder and guiding me up the stairs to the front door.

There was a small entryway and then a large room filled with old furniture.

"The Lakewood was one of the most desirable tourist houses in its day," Louise told Sanford. She went on to explain how the resort business had died and how she and her husband, Gordon, had decided to use the property as a group foster home. She didn't have any children of her own, "but I always consider my wards my own," she added.

We went upstairs and stopped at a room that was half the size of my room at the Delorice residence.

"I just cleaned it thoroughly. The girls share the bathroom across the hall," Louise explained. "Cooperation is the key word here," she told Sanford. "It prepares them for life."

Sanford smiled again. He set my suitcases down.

"Well," Louise said, looking at him and then at me. "Why don't I give you two time to say good-bye and then I'll show Janet around the house."

"Thank you," Sanford said.

She left us and I sat on what was to be my bunk. He stood there silently for a moment.

"Oh, I wanted you to have some money," he began, and dug into his pocket to produce a billfold and pulled out some large bills. I started to shake my head. "No, please, take it and hide it," he insisted. "First chance you get, put it in the bank. Having a little money of your own will give you some independence, Janet." He forced the money into my hand. "You won't be here long," he said, looking around. "You're a very talented, beautiful child."

I didn't know what to say to him.

"Well, maybe I'll look in on you from time to time. Would you like that?"

I shook my head and he looked surprised.

"You wouldn't? Why not?"

"When you get old, you lose your memory," I said, "so you won't remember what you can't have anymore."

He stared at me and smiled.

"Who told you that?"

I shrugged. "Nobody. I thought it up one day."

"You're probably right. It's nature's way. But I hope you don't forget me, Janet. I won't forget you."

"Celine's already forgotten me," I said.

"She's just mixed you up with memories of herself," he said.

"Then it's better she forgets."

He looked like he was going to cry. All he had ever done before was kiss me softly on the forehead and hold my hand crossing streets. He went to his knees this time and embraced me, holding me to him for a moment.

"I wanted a daughter like you, more than anything," he whispered. Then he kissed me on the cheek and stood up quickly, turned, and walked out of the room. I listened to his footsteps descending the stairway.

For a long moment I just sat there staring at the floor. Finally I went to the window and looked down and saw his car disappear down the road. I started to cry, the first tear exploding in a hot drop to trickle down my cheek, when suddenly a beautiful butterfly landed on the windowsill. It lingered for a moment and then lifted into the wind. I watched it flutter away and I thought, someday, that will be me.

Pocket Books
Proudly Presents

CRYSTAL

V. C. ANDREWS

**The Spellbinding Second Novel
in the New Orphans Series**

**Turn the page for a preview of
Crystal . . .**

One night Mr. Philips forgot his keys. It was as simple as that. Even though I was just a little over eleven, I had been helping in the administrative office as usual, filing purchase orders, receipts, and repair orders. I had left Molly Stuart's watch in Mr. Philips's bathroom when I had taken it off to wash my hands. I didn't have a watch and she let me borrow hers once in a while. When she saw I didn't have it on my wrist, she asked me about it and I remembered. This was after supper, when we were all in our rooms doing homework. I told her not to worry. I knew where it was. She fumed and fumed until blood flooded her face. She was positive someone would have stolen it by now because Mr. Philips's office door was never locked. So I left my room and hurried downstairs. I entered, put on the lights, and looked in the bathroom. There it was on the sink where I had left it.

I turned to leave and that was when I saw Mr. Philips's keys on his desk. I knew they were the keys to the secret files, the files that held information about each of us. Other kids were always asking me if I had ever seen the files out while I was working there. I never had.

My heart skipped a beat. I looked at the door and back at those magical keys. It was close to impossible for an orphan to learn about his or her biological past, at least until he or she turned eighteen. All I had ever been told was that my mother had been too sick to keep me and that I had no father.

I had never done a dishonest thing in my life, but this was different, I thought. This was not stealing. This was merely taking something that really belonged to me: knowledge about my own past. Quietly, I closed the front door and then I went to the desk, picked up the keys, and found the one that would open the drawers containing the secret files.

Funny, how I stood there, afraid to touch the file that had my name on its tab. Was I afraid to break a rule or afraid to learn about myself? Finally, I got up enough nerve and pulled out my file. It was thicker than I had imagined it could be. I turned off the office lights so I wouldn't attract any attention and sat on the floor by the bathroom with the door only slightly ajar. A thin shaft of light escaped and provided enough illumination for me to read the pages.

The first few were filled with information I already knew about myself: medical history, school records; but the bottom stack of pages opened the dark doors of my past and revealed information that both surprised and frightened me.

According to what I read, my mother, Amanda Perry, had been diagnosed as a manic depressive when she was only in her midteens. She was institutionalized at seventeen after repeated efforts to commit suicide, once cutting her wrists and twice trying to overdose with sleeping pills.

I read on and learned that while my mother was in a mental facility, she was impregnated by an attendant. Apparently, they never knew which attendant, so I realized that some degenerate out there was my father, unless I wanted to believe my mother and this attendant had the most romantic and wonderful love affair between her drug therapies, cold baths, and electric shock treatments.

Anyway, by the time they had realized my mother was pregnant, someone made the official decision not to abort me. After I was born, obviously neither my paternal nor my maternal grandparents wanted anything to do with me, and Mr. Degenerate Attendant wasn't going to come out and claim me, so I was immediately made a ward of the state. My reports didn't say who had named me Crystal. I like to think it was the one and only thing my poor mother had been able to give me. I had nothing else, not even the slightest idea who I was, until I managed to sneak into these files.

I saw a simple statement about my mother's death at the age of twenty-two. Her last attempt at taking her own life was a successful one. I would never meet her, even years from now when I was on my own.

I remember the revelations made my hands shake and gave me a hollow feeling at the base of my stomach. Would I inherit my mother's mental problems? Would I inherit my father's evil ways? After I put the file back, locked up the cabinet, returned the keys to the desk, and left, I had to go right to the bathroom because I felt like I had to throw up.

I managed to keep my supper down but washed my face with cold water just to calm myself. When I looked in the mirror then, I studied myself, searching my eyes, my mouth, looking for some sign of evil. I felt like Dr. Jekyll searching for a glimpse of Mr. Hyde. From that day forward I've had nightmares about it. In them I see myself become mentally ill and so sick that I would be put in some clinic and locked away forever.

I suppose it was just natural that any psychologist who knew my past would wonder if I shared any characteristics with my parents. From what I had read, I understood that my mother apparently acted out in school often and was a very difficult student for all the teachers. She was constantly in trouble. I've never been like that, but I recently read that this sort of behavior is considered a call for help, just as attempting suicide is.

With all these calls for help, the world seemed like a great big ocean with many people drowning and lifeguards whimsically choosing to help this one or that one. Naturally, the richer ones always were saved or at least tossed a lifeline. Those like me were shoved into mental institutions, group foster homes, orphanages, and prisons. We were swept under the rug with so many others. It made me wonder how anyone could walk on it.

I never told anyone what I had learned, of course, but I began to understand why it was that few prospective parents ever showed interest in me. They probably were given information about my past and decided not to take a chance on someone like me.

Once, when I was at a different orphanage, I was sitting outside and reading *The Diary of Anne Frank*. (I was always two or three reading grade levels above other kids my age.) Suddenly, I felt a shadow move over me and I looked up to see a balloon drifting in the wind, the string dangling like a tail. Some little boy or girl had loosened their grip and it had escaped. Now, however, it drifted aimlessly, attached to no one, doomed never to return to its owner. It disappeared over a rim of treetops and I thought, that's what we're all like here, balloons that someone released willingly or unwillingly, poor souls lost and sailing into the wind, waiting and hoping for another hand to take hold of us and bring us back to earth.

Three more years went by without my being adopted or given a foster home. I was still helping Mr. Philips in his office, and about a year ago, he started calling me Little Miss Efficiency. I didn't mind it, even when he used me to rankle his assistants. He's always said things like, "Why can't you be as responsible or as careful as Crystal?" He even said that occasionally to his secretary, Mrs. Mills.

Mrs. Mills always looked like she was drowning in carbon copies. Her fingers were usually blue or black because of ribbons, ink cartridges, toner she had to change. In the morning she came to work looking as well put together as a work of classical art, not a strand of her blue-gray hair out of place, her makeup perfect, her clothing clean and unwrinkled, but by the end of the day, her bangs were always dangling over her eyes, her blouse usually had a smudge somewhere on it, maybe two, and her lipstick had somehow spread onto a cheek, and she had become a work of abstract art. I know she's one person who never resented me. She was always happy to greet me and appreciated the work I did, work she would probably have had to do otherwise.

For someone my age, I know a lot about human psychology. I got interested in it after I read about my mother. Now I'm thinking I might be a doctor someday, and anyway, it's good to know as much as you can about psychology. It comes in handy, especially around orphanages.

But it's not always an asset to be smarter than other people or more responsible. This is especially true for orphans. The more helpless you seem, the better your chances are for being adopted. If you look like you can take care of yourself, who wants you? At least, that's another one of my theories for why I was a prisoner of the system for as long as I was. Prospective adoption parents don't like feeling inferior to the child they might adopt. I've seen it firsthand.

There was this couple who asked specifically for me. They wanted a child who was older. The woman whose name was Chastity had a silly little grin on her face. Her husband called her Chas and she called him Arn, short for Arnold. I suppose they would have ended up calling me Crys. Completing words was difficult for them. They had the same problem with sentences, always leaving a part dangling, like when Chas asked me, "What do you want to be when you . . ."

"When I what?" I forced her to say.

"Get older. Graduate from . . ."

"College or high school or the armed services or secretarial school or computer training?" I cataloged. I had taken an immediate dislike to them. She giggled too much and he looked like he wanted to be someplace else the moment he walked into the room.

"Yes," she said, giggling.

"I suppose I want to be a doctor, but I might want to be a writer. I'm not absolutely sure. What do you want to be?" I asked her and she batted her eyelashes with a smile of utter confusion.

"What?"

"When you . . ." I looked at Arn and he smirked.

Her smile wilted like a flower and gradually evaporated completely. Her eyes were forbidding and soon filled with a nervous energy. I couldn't count how many times she gazed longingly at the door.

They looked quite relieved when the interview ended. I didn't have another interview until just a week ago, but I was happy to met Thelma and Karl Morris. Apparently, my background didn't frighten them, nor did my being precocious annoy them. In fact, afterward, Mr. Philips told me I was exactly what they wanted: an adolescent who promised to be no problem, who wouldn't make a major demand on their lives, who had some independence, and who was in good health.

Thelma seemed convinced that whatever damage she believed I'd suffered as an orphan would be corrected after a few weeks of life in her and Karl's home. I loved her cockeyed optimism. She was a small woman in her late twenties with very curly light brown hair and hazel eyes that were as bright and innocent as a six-year-old's.

Karl was only a few inches taller, with thin dark brown hair and dull brown eyes. He looked much older, but was only in his early thirties. He had a soft, friendly smile that settled in his pudgy face like berries in cream. He was stout. His hands were small, but his fingers were thick.

He was an accountant and she said she was a housewife, but they had long ago decided that was a job too and she should be paid a salary for it. She had even gotten raises when they had good years. They couldn't stop talking about themselves. It was as if they wanted to get out their entire lives in one meeting.

The best thing I could say about them was that there was absolutely nothing subtle, contrived, or threatening about them. What you saw was what you got. I liked that. It made me feel at ease. At times during the interview, it was more like I was there to decide if I would adopt them.

"Everything is just too serious here," Thelma told me toward the end of our session. She grimaced, folding her mouth into a disapproving frown. "It's just too serious a place for a young person to think of as any sort of home. I don't hear any laughter. I don't see any smiles."

Then she suddenly grew very serious herself and leaned toward me to whisper. "You don't have a boyfriend yet, do you? I'd hate to break up a budding romance."

"Hardly," I told her. "Most of the boys here are quite immature." She liked that and was immediately relieved.

"Good," she said, "then it's settled. You'll come home with us and we'll never speak of anything unpleasant again. We don't believe in sadness—if you don't think about the bad things in life, you'll find they all just go away—you'll see."

I should have known what that meant, but for once in my short life, I decided to stop analyzing everyone and just enjoy the company of someone, especially someone who wanted to be my mother.

POCKET
BOOKS

THE ORPHANS SERIES
THE NEW VIRGINIA ANDREWS ®

Coming soon…

CRYSTAL
Book 2

When the Morrises choose Crystal from all the girls and
boys in the orphanage, she is full of optimism – at last
she has a home to call her own. Karl Morris, her new
dad, likes maths as much as she likes science, and he's
already proud of her being a good student. Thelma, her
new mom, makes her feel truly wanted for the first time.
And though Thelma seems more interested in her
television soap operas than in real life, Crystal feels that
their tidy little house will become a real home.
Crystal is especially pleased when the Morrises approve
of her first boyfriend. But she will soon discover that in
her new home, sadness is banished to the back of a
closet… and that means no one is prepared when a
shocking tragedy comes rattling at the door.

0 671 02198 2

£2.99

POCKET
B O O K S

THE ORPHANS SERIES
THE NEW VIRGINIA ANDREWS ®

Coming soon...

BROOKE
Book 3

In Brooke's most secret dreams, her mother would
return to the orphanage, full of remorse for having left
her there so long ago. Brooke never imagined a rich
couple who looked like movie stars would want her to
be their daughter. Yet Pamela and Peter Thompson seem
thrilled to welcome her to her huge, gleaming house.
Soon Brooke is receiving daily lessons in etiquette, every
hour and every outfit is planned to prepare her for the
beauty pageants Pamela demands that she enter and
win. But Brooke just wants to play on the school softball
team, where her real talents are appreciated. For only
when she's on the field with her friends can she escape
the dreadful feeling that she must always be
obedient...or risk losing her golden chance for a name, a
home and freedom from the terrible secrets of her past.

0 671 02195 8
£2.99

POCKET
B O O K S

THE ORPHANS SERIES
THE NEW VIRGINIA ANDREWS ®

Coming soon...

RAVEN
Book 4

Living with her drunken mother in a battered apartment
hardly fit for humans, Raven often hears how her birth
twelve years ago was a big mistake. Then her mother is
arrested, and her Uncle Reuben takes Raven to live with
him, her aunt and two cousins. Aunt Clara welcomes her
warmly, and for the first time Raven has her own room
in a clean, orderly household. In spite of Uncle Reuben's
strict rules and cruel comments, as she falls asleep on her
own soft pillow she feels in her heart a faint tremor of
hope.
But while she knows that Uncle Reuben prefers not to
have her there, Raven cannot guess at the shocking
secrets lurking beneath the family's ordinary facade...or
anticipate the painful humiliation that will make her
wish for her old life with Mama again...

0 671 02196 6
£2.99

POCKET
B O O K S

THE ORPHANS SERIES
THE NEW VIRGINIA ANDREWS ®

And finally... The four orphans together at last!

RUNAWAYS

In the grim foster home for orphans run by Louise and
Gordon Tooey, at least Brooke, Crystal, Raven and
Butterfly had each other. Calling themselves 'sisters',
together they could forget the past and dream of a new
chance... a real home. Then they discovered a secret even
more haunting than Gordon's boots pounding on the
wooden floors. Their fragile hopes of a better life
shattered, they escaped the only way they could. Soon
they were runaways in a borrowed car, desperately
wishing to wake up one morning in a place of sunshine
and love.
But the highway is a dangerous place, and soon they
were penniless and more vulnerable than ever. Alone
under the wide western sky, they had only each other to
ask if they should give up their dreams... of if they were
really halfway to a haven of safety and happiness.

0 684 85173 3
£16.99